ONLY A LADY WILL DO

TO MARRY A ROGUE, BOOK 5

COPYRIGHT

ONLY A LADY WILL DO

TO MARRY A ROGUE, BOOK 5

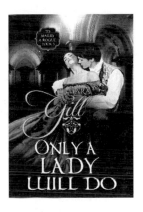

She's exactly what he isn't looking for...and everything he never knew needed...

Josh Worthingham, Duke of Penworth, must marry—and not just any bride will do. He needs a true lady to be his duchess. It's what's expected of him, and he can accept no less. So, why is it that the only woman who snags his full attention is the entirely inappropriate Miss Iris Cooper?

Iris may be the granddaughter of an Earl, but that's where her lofty connections to the ton end. She knows securing a good match won't be easy—especially not when she still carries the scars of her failed first union. There's no way the Duke of Penworth can ever be hers. But a girl can dream, can't she?

Can a stolen kiss in a drawing room turn Iris's dreams into reality? Or will their differences—and the dark secret Josh is harboring—destroy their one chance at happily ever after?

CHAPTER 1

London 1812

*H*ow had he managed to get himself into this mess? Josh Worthingham, Duke of Penworth, lowered his head and tried to use the ferns and abundant greenery his mother had placed around their London home for the ball to shield his location. She had been adamant that she wanted the room to represent the delightful outdoors, the trees, moss, grasses, and flowers that grew in the parklands about their estate, Dunsleigh.

His mother had pulled off the effect, and it was stunning. If not a little over the top for Josh's liking, but the foliage did at least enable him to hide.

The guests too gasped and smiled, looked about with awe, just what his mother would adore, being this was her final year as the Duchess of Penworth, a celebration for her time as one of the pillars of society. One must go out with a bang if one was to be remembered.

Not that his mother was going too far, but it was due to his declaration that this Season he would marry. Find a wife suitable for the role of a duchess and let his mother hand over the busy reins of her position in society.

He could only hope the colossal mistake he'd made last year in Hampshire did not follow him to town. He caught sight of Lady Sophie and cringed. Being respectable and kind did not mean he would offer the hand of marriage. He had shown such respect to many ladies over the years and had not proposed. Why the rumor he would ask Lady Sophie had arisen, he could not fathom, nor would he allow it to continue.

When had the rules changed? He had danced and had discourse with many ladies during his years scuffing the boards in London. When had talking and dancing morphed into his choice of bride?

An absurd notion.

He caught sight of Lady Sophie, surrounded by her many beaus, but he did not wish to be one of them. At one time, she may have piqued his interest, but that had long passed. Nor had he ever shown more interest than a gentleman should. His mother had raised him right, and he was one duke who did not bend the rules.

There was something about the lady he did not like, a littleness to her that was ugly no matter how beautiful she was. No amount of rouge or diamonds could alter one's personality if it were rotten at its core.

A finger flicked his ear, and he started. His older sister Elizabeth laughed, coming to stand at his side. "Still hiding, I see. We have been in London for a month, Josh darling. I think it is time you came out of the shadows and faced the lady who seems to be telling all of London how enamored you are of her. Of course, she's only telling a select few of her friends so the rumor does not spread too far and wide, but it would seem it has scattered to Mama's ears at least."

Josh groaned, hating that he would have to flee the

Season if he could not find a way out of this mess. Maybe Elizabeth would like him to travel north to Scotland and check on their estate while they were in London this year.

"It is a mess that I cannot escape. I danced with her in Hampshire and conversed as one would since they were hosting the ball. How can a lady from that form the opinion that a proposal is imminent?" He met his sister's amused gaze and frowned. Was no man safe from such women? Was this how the ladies thought to trap men into their marriage nets?

Well, he would not succumb to such antics. He would choose his lady when he found one suitable for the position as duchess.

Not just any lady would do.

Oh no, his lady needed to be witty, intelligent, and beautiful if he could be so vain to desire such a thing. But most of all, she needed to be from an upstanding family, without reproach, without a blemish to her name, and a sizable dowry. Not that he needed such funds, but he did not want to be one of those fathers who left everything to his eldest son and had nothing for his other children. His parents had bestowed fortunes on all their children, and he wanted to do the same.

"You must have made an impression in Hampshire." Elizabeth sipped her negus, watching the throng of guests behind the green foilage with him. "You must also stop hiding, return to the ball and speak with all manner of ladies and gentlemen to quell the rumors. While I would not suggest avoiding Lady Sophie at all costs, I think asking another of her friends to dance and not paying too much attention to the lady, would be wise. I'm certain by acting so, all this nonsense will soon pass, and there will be another bet at Whites that does not include you."

He groaned. "You know of the bet?" How he loathed that

book and the trouble it wrought. Not just this Season, but in the past. And at his own doing.

Fool.

Elizabeth raised a dubious brow. "Of course, does not everyone?"

That was probably also true. His good friend Anthony, Earl Thetford had thought it a lark in making a bet at his expense. Who would be the lady the Duke of Penworth marries? Several names were listed, Lady Sophie's with the best odds. None of them would be the woman he married. He had not found her as yet. His sisters had married for love. He knew that to his very core. The way they looked at their spouses reminded him of how his mama once looked at his father before he passed.

He wanted that for himself. To marry was for life, and he did not want to regret his choice should it be wrong, for there would be no changing it after the fact.

"That book ought to be burned for all the trouble it's caused many families in London."

Elizabeth threw him a curious look but did not pry into his thoughts. "Did you hear," she said, changing the subject, "that Mama is going to be sponsoring her closest friend's daughter this Season? She could not make it tonight but will be here tomorrow."

Josh inwardly groaned, having heard already. A vicar's daughter whose mother had been born a daughter of an earl but married beneath her station and reportedly was shunned by her family for her efforts in love.

He knew his mama had debuted with the young woman's mother the same year, and their friendship had remained one of the pen since the family never came to town.

"I did hear she was to arrive tomorrow. I will relocate to my bachelor lodgings for the duration of her stay, which I hope will not be long. The sooner she is married, the better."

"Be kind to her, Josh. You have always been a loving brother. I hope you will assist in finding a suitable match for the lady and not scuttle away at your club and gambling dens while she's here in town. She has not had an easy life, from what I have heard. You need to be kind."

He could no sooner be cruel to his sisters or his mama's sponsor, even if he wished to. It was not in his nature to be an ass. "I promised Mama I would escort them several times a week to any balls or musical events, operas, and such. I shall do the pretty and vet any suitors who step forward for her hand. I will ensure she marries well."

Elizabeth threw him a shrewd glance. "You will need all our assistance if she's to wed well. She will have nothing but her wits, charm, and looks to win her a match with no dowry or title. Let us hope she has all three in abundance."

"The Countess Buttersworth, her grandmother, will not wish to guide her? Surely, after all these years, she could not still be angry at her only daughter marrying a vicar?"

Elizabeth finished her drink and handed it off to a passing footman. "Mama heard the countess is quite put out that her granddaughter will be back in town. She had a Season several years ago, but it was not successful. I do not know all the particulars, but Mama said the countess is set to give her the cut direct."

Lady Buttersworth was an old, cranky witch. Who could treat family with such cruelness? "I trust in Mother's choice of friends. If she is fond of this young woman and her mother, I'm certain she will make a match. With or without her grandmother's help."

"And what of your life, dear brother? When shall I be able to welcome a duchess as my new sister? Will it be this year, you think? Another rumor surrounding you says that it will be."

Josh rubbed his jaw, thinking over his sister's words. No

doubt his mother had told his siblings of his statement. "I am set on finding a suitable bride for the position of duchess this Season. I have decided she must be a lady of the finest breeding, well-spoken and educated, and above all else, take London by storm with her beauty and grace."

Elizabeth snorted, covering her lapse in manners with a cough that Josh did not buy for one second. "How lovely. I wish you all the very best in finding this gem." She started off toward where their mama stood but turned before gaining too much distance. "Perhaps you ought to go fishing and catch a mermaid, dear brother. I'm certain you shall have more luck in finding one of those mythical creatures than the one you just mentioned."

Josh gaped before shutting his mouth with a snap. His idea for a bride was no mythical being. Why, his perfect lady could be here tonight, hiding in the greenery like him.

He stepped out of his hiding place, determined to find his jewel and crown her with a ducal coronet. The Season was young, and so was he, and he would prove his sister wrong and enjoy throwing his perfect bride before her when he found his match.

Cornwall

"Come here, you little." Iris reached for the piglet but missed the little mite. It scuttled away into the pen just as her foot caught on the trough. With a splat and a yelp, she landed facedown in pig filth.

"Damn you. I'm so going to enjoy eating you this evening," she mumbled, lifting herself. The stench of pig excrement, of rotten scraps from their home, made her eyes water. She kneeled, using the fence to pull herself upright, and tried again. The pig was fast, and with her limp, she was slower than the little animal but more determined than ever to catch him.

"Have you caught the piglet yet, darling? Cook wants to put it in the oven in the next hour, or it'll not be ready for your going-away dinner this evening."

Iris groaned, staring heavenward. London. She shuddered at the thought of traveling there, being courted by those money-hungry swains whom she had not an ounce of interest in. Nor did she have the money to tempt them into marrying a cripple.

Not after what had happened the first time she had traveled to town. Seven years ago now, full of hopes and dreams. How they had come crashing down, along with herself, leaving her lame and with a hideous scar along her temple to her eyebrow.

Dudley, Baronet Redgrove, her late betrothed.

Iris pushed the painful memory aside, looking for the piglet and finding it staring at her. Its little chest rose and fell rapidly, and its frightened eyes gave her pause.

She turned about, opening the gate to the pen and leaving the little animal alone. They could have something else for dinner this evening. She could not bring herself to kill the poor little creature, no matter what her mother said about the fact.

She kicked off the mud and dung from her boots and dress as she started for the well at the back of the vicarage.

She would also probably have to strip down to her shift before her mama let her indoors too.

"Where is the piglet?" her mama asked, hands on hips, an apron wrapped about her waist with all sorts of grime and food wiped onto it. Iris's lips lifted at the sight of her mama, an earl's daughter and heiress once upon a time. Should her grandmother, the Countess Buttersworth, see her only daughter now, she would drop dead at the sight of her, Iris was sure.

Her mama seemed to think it was her place to bother their cook in the kitchen, even though she was a terrible cook herself. The daughter of an earl had never stepped foot in the kitchens back at their estate in Derbyshire and had to learn how to boil water. Her mama had married for love and had adjusted her life to suit her heart and her husband's career in the church. She was a good woman, and Iris was determined to be just like her if she could.

"In the pen. I cannot catch it. We shall have to eat the chicken the Smiths brought around yesterday for us."

Her mama came out to the well, helping her haul up a pale of water. "What are we going to do with you, Iris? You cannot travel to London smelling like manure. We will have to bathe you overnight in vinegar to get the stench out," she said, undoing the buttons on the back of her gown.

When they had the bucket atop the stone well wall, Iris washed off as much grime and pig pen as possible. "You could always allow me to stay here. I am more than willing to find a quiet country squire to marry. I do not have to travel all those miles to find a suitable gentleman. And do not forget, my lame hip will thank you for it if I do not."

Her mama reached out, washing a little spot of God-knows-what from her cheek, a sadness in her clear, blue eyes. "You deserve so much, my darling—more than a country squire. You deserve to have the Season that was stolen from you. Now that you are well enough, the time has come to have you married, settled and happy. Let me do this for you."

"But does it have to be with the Duchess of Penworth that I have my Season? I do not want to be a burden to them."

"You will not be a burden. The duchess is so excited to have you this year. She is a lovely woman and friend. You will not be disappointed. I wish I could be with you, but with our position here in the parish, the people need us. You, my dear, do not. You are an intelligent, beautiful woman who has the world at her feet. I think you shall take London by storm."

Or she wouldn't, and merely hobble through the streets like an old cripple she felt she was at times. "I barely know the duchess. What if she does not like me?"

"She will love you, for she loves me. Our friendship is strong, and she does not have an unkind bone in her body. All her daughters are married now, and she welcomes having company in her townhouse this Season. Now, come, my dear. You shall need to bathe before dinner, and we cannot keep you up too late. You have a long journey before you."

Iris decided not to debate the subject any further to stay here in Cornwall, which wasn't something she should pursue. Her mama was determined, and as an earl's daughter to her very core, she usually gained her way.

But something told Iris that when it came to her taking London by storm, of being the success they believed she would be, that her parents were seeing her through rose-colored glasses. She was no gem. She was scarred inside and out; no doubt one who would be mocked over the next several months by those without empathy. Her time for a future had passed. She had buried all her hopes seven years ago with Dudley.

CHAPTER 2

*J*ris took the footman's hand, needing the assistance to climb down from the carriage after the last several hours on the road. The trip from Cornwall had taken several days. She'd had to stay an extra night at an inn due to her leg cramping up over the many hours sedate in a carriage.

Even now, it ached, and she rubbed the upper bone in her leg where it had fractured several years ago. She supposed she ought to be relieved that it had not broken entirely, or so the doctor had stated.

She stood on the flagstones before the Duke of Penworth's London residence. Her home for the next three months of the Season. The house was one of the largest in London, having a private driveway and fencing along the street front.

Flowers and hedges lined the front walls of the home. The house could not look more opposing to how Iris was in life. It was orderly and well-kept. She was none of those things, and a little niggle of dread settled in her belly that she would not be good enough to escort the duchess. To be part of their family for the next few months.

Would the duchess still wish to sponsor her this Season when she saw her charge was not as perfect as so many other ladies present in London?

Rumor had it the beautiful Lady Sophie from Hampshire was the belle of every ball. It was said that the Duke of Penworth himself had taken an interest in her prior to the Season.

The front door opened, and a liveried footman came down the stairs, giving her his arm. "The duchess is in the front drawing room, Miss Cooper. She charged me in bringing you to her."

Iris smiled at the young man, thankful for the support up the many steps. Normally she would not struggle, but the sedentary hours had left her sore and stiff. After a nice cup of tea and a comfortable chair that did not rock or drop into every pothole the wheel could find, she would be better.

"Thank you. That is very kind."

They walked up the stairs, and she gaped at the sight of the interior of the home. Marble and polished wood floors, magnificent paintings, some as large as several walls at the vicarage, hung all over the home. Opulent flower arrangements sat on several sideboards, and the foyer itself smelled like a sweet hothouse.

They made their way across the room, the sweeping staircase leading up to the first floor, a piece of art in itself.

She knew her mama had come from a similar home as the duchess, being an earl's daughter and she couldn't help but wonder if they were alike.

They entered a room of soft yellow with wood paneling on the lower quarter of the walls. Three cream settees hugged the fire burning in the grate, and a woman she'd never met before stood, a welcoming smile on her aged but attractive face.

"Iris, how lovely for you to be here. I have been so looking forward to your visit."

The duchess's warm smile quelled some of her misgivings. Her Grace stood, arms outstretched, before pulling Iris into a warm embrace.

The footman bowed and left, leaving them alone.

"Forgive me. I'm Sarah Worthingham, the Duchess of Penworth, but just as your dear mama always has, you may call me Sarah." The duchess reached up, taking Iris's face in her hands and studying her. "You look like your mama when she was your age. How lovely to meet you.

Iris remembered to dip into a curtsy. "Thank you for having me, Your Grace. I'm honored to be here. I cannot tell you how thankful I am that you've sponsored me."

The duchess waved her concerns aside and walked her over to a settee. Iris sank onto the seat, biting back a sigh of delight at the comfortable chair that would help with her aching bones.

"Dearest Jane, I could never refuse her, and as I'm certain she has already informed you, all my daughters are now married. My youngest just this past year."

Iris did know all of this. She glanced about the room, this space, too, very homey and welcoming. Not cold at all, which she had heard some affluent families tended to prefer when it came to their furnishings. "I wish them very happy." Iris all but purred when a footman brought in a steaming pot of tea and almond biscuits. How long since she'd had a lovely cup of tea in a comfortable chair and not awful hours of travel still ahead of her?

The duchess thanked the footman but dismissed him, preferring to pour the tea herself. "Do you have milk or sugar, my dear?"

"Both please," she answered, taking the cup and saucer when it was ready. "Thank you." Iris relaxed at the duchess's ease and welcoming disposition. She hoped that it would remain so. "Mama sends her regards, and I have a letter in my trunk for you that she charged me with delivering when I arrived."

"Wonderful," the duchess said, smiling brightly. "Jane's letters are always entertaining."

Iris found herself smiling in return, hope blossoming in her chest that perhaps the Season in town would not be so very bad. Not with the Duchess of Penworth at her side. Her time in town several years ago had been a disaster, and she did not want anything of the same to occur again.

The duchess sipped her tea, taking in her carriage dress. Iris believed it had too much frogging on it to be fashionable. A little gaudy for her style. "You will need new gowns, and we shall start shopping for them tomorrow. I'm certain we shall be able to have several delivered before your first ball this Friday, but until then, you may wear whatever your maid has packed for you. I'm certain they will do very well for the time being."

Iris's eyes went wide. Several gowns? "How many gowns do you suppose I shall require, Your Grace?"

"Please, call me Sarah. I insist. And you shall have at least ten ballgowns to start. We shall have more made as the Season continues. You will have your morning gowns, evening wear, and ballgowns. And then let us not forget you will need all new shifts, stays, petticoats, stockings, and shoes. A hat for the different occasions and events we're to attend. A parasol and gloves. And if you're fortunate to gain an offer of marriage, which after seeing you, my dear, I do believe will be forthcoming in the weeks ahead, you will need new night rails, a dressing gown, and wrappers."

The idea of so many clothes, the many balls and parties

she would have to attend muddled her senses. She could only hope her leg would not cause too much strife at having to dance so much and stand for several hours at a time.

As if sensing her unease, the duchess set her cup down, settling her hands in her lap in a businesslike manner. "I knew of your carriage accident several years ago. Your mama informed me of it when it happened. I did visit you when you were taken ill, but you probably do not remember."

Iris did not remember that day at all. Well, that wasn't exactly true. She remembered figments of it, but only leading up to being picked up by Dudley before their turn in Hyde Park. After that, the day was eliminated from her memory. She could recall waking up several days later, no longer betrothed and a cripple.

"I will not push you to dance if you do not feel up to it, and we shall always have a comfortable chair to sit in when the need arises. I want this Season to be pleasant for you, dear. Successful too. You deserve as much happiness as my children have found with their respective life partners, and I'm determined to find you yours."

Relief poured through her at knowing the duchess would be considerate of her lameness. "Thank you, Your..." she cleared her throat, testing out the familiarity the duchess wanted for the first time, "Sarah, for your kindness. I do wish to enjoy myself. It has been so very long since I have been in town, and although several of my friends are married now, it will be nice to see them again if they are here."

"Wonderful. There is a writing desk in your room, and if you give your letters to our butler, he shall have them posted posthaste."

Iris finished her tea, picking up a biscuit and taking a bite. She bit back a moan of delight at the sweetness that spread across her tongue. It would seem the cook the duchess employed was also marvelous.

"I understand that your son the duke is still unwed. Is he in town this Season?"

The duchess's eyes brightened with affection at the mention of her child. "He is indeed, and he will be here with us for your first ball. He's had to travel down to our estate in Surrey but will return before Friday. I hope you do not mind, but I have secured his assistance, and he is here to ensure your Season is an enjoyable one and successful. A dance with a duke always makes a lady more popular, and so I'm determined that you shall be the most sought-after young woman in the *ton*. You will have your choice of gentleman to take your hand in marriage, but with copious amounts to choose from, I'm hoping you shall find the man who stops your heart at the very sight of him. A love match will only do."

Iris inwardly sighed at how delightful that sounded while a pang of sadness also followed the emotion. Poor Dudley, the silly fool did not deserve such an ending. He too should be happily married, and to her. She wondered for a moment if they would have had children by now. Would they have been happy? All an unknown and forever to be that way since he was gone and she was back in London, searching for a new fiancé.

"You do not think my injury will put me at a disadvantage? Walking can become difficult sometimes. I have a small limp when the weather is chilly, and the scar does not help," she said, pointing to the cut across her temple and brow.

"None of that will matter, my dear. Not to a man who is genuine of character and in love with you. While I do not doubt your troubles are vexing, your difficulties do not impede your happiness. The scar is nothing at all, and we shall not overtax you so that you are pained to walk or dance. All will be well, my dear. I will ensure it is so."

"Thank you, Sarah. I do not know how I shall ever repay you such kindness."

The duchess waved her thanks aside, picking up an almond biscuit also. "Jane is my friend, and this is no trouble at all. I enjoy the Season and will enjoy having you, the daughter of my closest friend, under my roof for several months. I am in my element, my dear. No thanks necessary."

CHAPTER 3

*J*osh strolled into his mother's private upstairs parlor, having just returned from Dunsleigh. The day was a beautiful spring morning. After returning late the evening before, he'd walked the short distance from his Albany bachelor rooms on Piccadilly to here on Hanover Square. The large Georgian manor house, taking up a good portion of the square, filled him with pride.

A home as precious to him as his country estate.

When his mother's sponsor was married and settled into her new life and out from under his mother's roof, he shall return home and bring his new wife with him—once he found her, of course.

Over the past several days, the short break from London had been welcome, especially when the matrons of the *ton* seemed to see him as the one bachelor who was perfect for their many daughters. A duke, ready to settle down, was a most-sought-after commodity.

His mother, he was certain, fanned the flames of such news, made the *ton* salivate at his eligibility. But he would choose whom he wanted beside him for the remainder of his days and no one else, of that he was most certain. His wife would be a lady of the finest quality, poise, and connections to rival his own. As Penworth, only the best would do for him.

Entering the home, he handed a waiting footman his greatcoat and hat and took the stairs two at a time, knowing he was late for tea his mama was holding to introduce him to the young woman she was sponsoring.

He had never met the young lady before, and he hoped she did not take up too much of his time in introducing her to society as he had his own plans to attend to this year. His own bride to find.

He checked his cravat and apparel, slicing a hand through his hair as he came up to the parlor door. Feminine voices and laughter met his ears. It reminded him of how his sisters laughed when they were among family. It pleased him that the young woman was settling in well, comfortable in the dowager duchess's presence, which some people were not.

Josh strolled into the room, spying his mama first. He smiled, bowing, and glanced to where he could see the other occupant. His heart stopped at the sight of her. Long, dark locks he'd pushed out of her face all those years ago to check if she were breathing. Even now, the acrid smell of blood teased his senses. There had been so much of it. He had never thought to see her again. How was it she was here? This could not be the woman his mother was sponsoring.

Good God, no. Please do not be her.

He pinned a smile to his lips, but nothing would halt the blood he felt draining from his face.

Miss Iris Cooper. It could not be.

The once-betrothed to Baronet Redgrove. A gentleman who ran about with him and others around London several years ago. Wild and reckless they had been. Stupid was more an accurate description. The woman, smiling in welcome, had paid the price for their madness. Well, at least his follies.

His eyes latched on to the scar on her face, the day she was gifted such a wound crashing down on him like a bookcase.

That she was injured at all could be lain at his door. Did she know who he was? Did she know it was his fault she was injured? He studied her features. Her sparkling, welcoming eyes said she did not. But women could be devious. Pretend all was well when it was not.

She clasped the side of the settee, struggling to stand before dipping into a curtsy, the tightness about her lips telling him the movement pained her.

"Your Grace, this is Miss Iris Cooper," his mama said, making the introductions.

He bowed, rallying himself to calm his beating heart. "Miss Cooper, welcome to our home. I hope your stay has been pleasant so far?"

His mother gestured for her to sit, and she seemed to welcome the ability to do so, a little sigh of relief passing her lips as she sat. "It has been wonderful so far. Your mama has been such a treasure sponsoring me so. My only concern is that you have been misplaced during my stay."

He shook his head, pouring himself a cup of tea and wishing it were something stronger. "My lodgings are more than comfortable and not too far. It is only a short walk to attend to the estate books every day. So you see, it is no trouble at all," he said, sipping his tea.

His mother watched him, and he could see she had noted his unease. He could only hope Miss Cooper did not recognize him. How she could not, however, he could not fathom.

"We're to attend Earl Clifford's ball this evening, my dear. Do not forget to pick us up in the family carriage at nine."

His mother threw him a pointed stare as if that would make him remember any better.

Not that he would forget. Not now, at least.

"You are the daughter of mama's favorite friend, I understand. Have you never been to town before?" he queried, needing to know how it was that she did not know who he was. Or how he had missed that Miss Iris Cooper was the woman his mother was sponsoring this season. Had he not been listening every time his mother prattled on about the young woman?

"Not for several years, Your Grace. I did have my first Season at eighteen and made a suitable match, but..." Miss Cooper's words wavered, and she cast a look at his mama, who nodded for her to continue. "There was a carriage accident in Hyde Park. I was thrown clear of the carriage, but my betrothed was not. He was killed, and I was severely injured. I returned home once I was healed."

"How terrible for you," he said, his voice brittle even to his own ears. "I'm very sorry that happened to you."

"Iris's mama is Lady Jane Buttersworth. She is known as Lady Jane still as she is the only daughter of the late Earl Buttersworth, and Countess Buttersworth."

Josh swallowed hard. Of course, Lady Jane. He had not connected her ladyship and Miss Cooper together or had simply forgotten the relationship. How arrogant of him to never have looked into Miss Cooper's health after returning home to Cornwall. He ought to be horsewhipped for being such an ass.

You are no longer so. You have changed your ways.

Still, he had been, and he could not forgive himself for his rash actions that put others at risk. Damn himself and his wild nature.

Not that Baron Redgrove was much better. The man was determined to take up every bet, every dare that came his way—always wanting to prove a point that he was better than everyone else. Josh ran a hand over his jaw, setting down his cup with more force than he meant to. It clattered, making his mama jump.

"Were you badly injured?" He knew she had been, but so caught up in his youthful folly, his inability to see past his greatness, he had not followed up on her progress. Never had he suspected she was the daughter of his mother's favorite friend.

"I fractured my thigh bone and scarred my face severely. I have no memory of the day at all, only the morning, which is vague at best. I do not remember much else but the pain and waking up several days later to the news that Dudley had passed, and I would return to Cornwall when I was healed. I have not been back to London since then, not until your mama invited me to stay, to have a second Season and one that will hopefully end on a happier note than my first."

Good God, he was going to hell. She had suffered memory loss and was also lame? Was that why to stand looked so painful to her? Her leg gave her grief even to this day?

Determination thrummed through him at the knowledge, and he would do all that he could to see her happily settled before the end of the Season to a good, kind man who would spoil and love her to the end of days.

"With Mother's help and my own, we shall have all your wishes fulfilled. The Season will be a success. I promise you that, Miss Cooper."

His mother's eyes widened, but she smiled, clearly delighted. "Thank you, dear. Your assistance and guidance on who would be a suitable match for Iris is just the thing we need. I know you will not steer her into anything that will end in unhappiness."

He smiled, resolved to make amends for his actions all

those years ago. Amends he should have made days after she regained consciousness. Fool that he was, he had not done so, but he would ensure she was happy and settled before he found his perfect match.

"It is no trouble at all. You are a friend of the family after all."

Miss Cooper smiled as he felt the breath in his lungs expel. It would not be at all troubling in gaining her a husband. Even with the scar that traveled from her temple to just above her eye, or the leg that pained her, she was a beautiful woman—dark, luxurious locks and large, almond-shaped eyes, lips that were pouty and kissable.

He shifted on his seat, unsure where that thought came from but determined to dismiss it. He had a lady to marry off to a good man. A pretty face would not divert him.

"I shall be here by nine as agreed. Until then, have a pleasant afternoon, ladies."

His mother waved him off, and as he walked down the passage, he could hear Miss Cooper's exciting words over the night to come.

Shame washed over Josh. How had he never checked on her person, on her wellbeing? Should his family find out how he had treated Miss Cooper, his hand behind the bet that injured her, or even the lady herself, he was certain his family or Iris would never forgive him. And rightfully so, for the act was unforgivable.

CHAPTER 4

*I*ris stood beside the Duchess of Penworth at the base of the front steps, waiting for the duke to arrive as agreed. The night air was fragrant with the many flowers that grew at the front of the London home, the wisteria strongest of them all.

Iris looked up at the sky, barely making out the stars. At home in Cornwall, the stars were in their millions, gifting those who cared to look up at their beauty. Not here in London, however. You could hardly see past the roofs.

"Ah, here he comes, my dear," the duchess said beside her, pulling her shawl closer about her shoulders.

Iris adjusted her stance, trying to alleviate her weight on her bad leg. Could there be a storm later this evening? It would certainly explain her aching leg that had not stopped hurting all day.

The duchess, having seen her struggles, had decided to gift her a walking cane. It was a delightful wooden one with a golden lion on its handle. The most ornate and pretty walking cane Iris had ever seen in her life, and she was quietly terrified she would misplace it.

The carriage rolled to a stop before them, and a footman ran to open the door. He held out his hand to help Her Grace climb up into the equipage and then Iris also.

Iris welcomed his help and settled herself beside the duchess. Only then did she take in the duke seated across from them, smiling in welcome.

"Good evening, Mother. Miss Cooper," the duke said, his deep gravelly voice making her inwardly sigh.

There was little denying the fact the duke was of exemplary looks, and this afternoon she had wracked her brain trying to remember if she had met him during her first Season.

They had not circulated in the same friendship sphere, certainly not up until she became engaged to the baron, but she did not think she had met him before that. Although she was familiar with his family, his mother in particular whom she had met several times, the duke had never been one of them.

She was happy to make his acquaintance now, and she hoped he did help her choose a husband who was both kind and suitable—loving if she could manage it with her concerns.

Tonight the duke was dressed in a black superfine coat and silver waistcoat with intricate silver thread weaved upon it. His cravat was tied into a ballroom knot, his buckskin breeches fitting his muscular legs like a second skin.

Iris swallowed and took to studying the Mayfair streets passing them by instead. The last thing she wanted him to think was that she was ogling him, sizing him up for herself.

She would never presume to reach so high. When she had been offered marriage by Baron Redgrove, with no dowry and a mother whose family had shunned her for her choice, she believed he was above her in station. Her mama soon put paid to such dismissing sniffs the *ton* bestowed upon Iris and her family.

Even so, Iris was no fool, and the woman who became the next Duchess of Penworth would be a diamond of the first water. Not paste, as Iris so often felt about herself. The duke would marry a woman of his rank, of wealth and connections. No matter how flattering it may feel to be loved by such a man, he would never look at her.

"A pleasant evening, is it not?" The duke's gaze settled on Iris, and a shiver of awareness ran through her when his attention dipped to her gown. "You look very beautiful this evening, Miss Cooper. I hope you have room for me on your dance card?" he asked her, a genial smile on his lips.

"If you like, Your Grace," Iris answered, enjoying the fact he would ask her but not letting herself believe in fairy tales. Men like the duke did not marry daughters of vicars. "I must thank you again for assisting me this Season. I know it is not ideal for you."

"Nonsense." His voice lightened, and he waved her concerns aside. "It is no trouble. I am here in London too, and if I can guide and support you in your quest to marry, then that is what I endeavor to do."

"Thank you, darling," the duchess said, throwing her son a warm smile. "You are very good to help us in this way."

The carriage ride to the Clifford Ball did not take long, and they were soon before the doors to the townhouse. The house was not as large or grand as the duke's, but it was familiar. Iris had been here several years before to a ball, not long before the accident occurred.

People milled outside. Others shuffled up the stairs to go indoors. The carriage rolled to a stop, and the duke, without waiting for a footman, jumped down, turning to assist them.

Iris waited for the duchess to disembark first before she reached for the duke's hand. She clasped it, stepping down using her good leg, and was thankful when she had both feet on the ground and had not tripped and made a fool of herself before everyone.

Several guests watched them, some of the younger ladies' eyes narrowing in contemplation on who she was and, no doubt, what she was doing with the Penworth and his mother.

She wanted to shout out to them all that she was doing nothing at all, merely letting him help her, so she did not make a fool of herself. That she was no competition and the duke would be all theirs soon enough and not hers. Not ever.

They paid their respects to the host, the duchess leading them to a set of seats beside a fire that burned halfway along one wall. At least when she was not dancing, she could sit and remain warm.

"We shall remain here, my dear, and wait for the gentlemen to come to you."

The duke stood to her side, and she felt his presence like her very own heartbeat. She wished he would move away, go and dance and not hover. His very nearness made thinking difficult, and she needed her wits about her if she were to find a genuine gentleman not troubled by her injuries.

"I shall fetch you both ratafia," the duke said, striding off into the throng and soon impossible to see with all the people present this evening.

"My son is right, Iris dear. I do not think you understand how very handsome you are."

Iris could no sooner believe that than she would think she was fully capable. The duchess was merely kind to her friend's daughter. "While my dress is beautiful and my hair has never been set so perfectly, I know that I am not all that I could be, but I thank you for the compliment."

"You, my dear, need to take a compliment and believe it when it is dealt. I am many things, but I do not speak untruths. You shine brighter than everyone else here. Believe that if nothing else."

Iris supposed that was true, but then, at times to believe the kind words of others was very hard to do. She could be so very hard on herself. "I do not recognize anyone here," she said, wanting to change the subject. "The girls I debuted with are long-married and settled, I suppose."

"The Season is young, and they may return to town over the next several weeks. I do hope you soon have some acquaintances. I should hate for you to grow bored and have to sit with me every ball."

"I shall never grow bored." The thought of doing so was impossible to fathom. The duchess had been wonderful so far, the duke too, caring and sweet. She could not ever be fatigued by the London Season.

"Do not feel that you must sit with me always. You may take a turn about the room, seek out conversation if you feel up to it."

"I thank you. I promise you I shall, but for tonight do you think it will be well if I sit here with you? If you do not mind, of course." With her leg paining her today, no doubt still annoyed after the many miles she traveled from Cornwall, to move about on top of dancing may be too much to bear.

The duchess reached across, patting her hand. "I do not mind in the least. You may take your time and seek out friendship when you are ready. However, I feel I should warn you that the late Baron Redgrove's cousin and heir is in London. Do you know him at all?"

Iris shook her head. "I do not, no." She had never met the man. All she knew was that Dudley's family had been saddened that the title had been lost, along with their son. Dudley's mother had never queried her parents on her well-being after the accident, and Iris had always felt Dudley's mother blamed her in a way for the tragedy that took her only son.

Not that it had been her fault. Dudley had been careless, or so witnesses had stated to her family after the fact. People had seen him racing around Hyde Park with her beside him, clutching on for dear life from all reports. Not that she remembered any of it and not that anything she did then or said now would change history.

"I do not think the new baron would know who I am, even if we were introduced."

"That is probably true," the duchess said, just as her son the duke returned.

Iris thanked His Grace for her drink and seated herself, relieved to be off her feet. Since she traveled from Cornwall, her leg had been giving her an awful time of it, and she hoped it settled down soon. She may be lame, but she did not particularly like everyone seeing her suffer from such effects.

The duke stood beside her, giving her the impression of a Roman statue guarding the vestal virgins. She sipped the sweet beverage, smiling to herself, but then as several gentlemen nodded in hello as they strolled past, none ventured to speak to her.

This was not a good start to her Season. Were they put off by the duke standing nearby, or the fact they knew of her wounds and did not want a wife that suffered from her injuries and was scarred from them?

She reached up, running her finger along the scar on her temple, hoping the small amount of white imperial powder that her maid had used this evening had concealed the scar somewhat.

The idea of being alone for the rest of her life was not something she wanted to contemplate. She had always wanted a husband and family to make a home as loving and fun as the one she grew up with.

The first strains of a waltz sounded, and the duke bowed before her, holding out his arm. "My dance, I believe, Miss Cooper," he said, his voice huskier than she'd heard it before. She swallowed the butterflies that his tone caused in her stomach and reached for his arm, grateful for his kindness. People had sought her company during her first Season. To now be a potential wallflower was not something she knew how to deal with.

"Thank you, Your Grace." The duke led her out onto the floor, and she could feel the eyes of the room upon her. She prayed some of them at least were male, and their interest was piqued.

*J*osh could feel the eyes of the *ton* boring into his back as he led Miss Cooper out onto the floor. She was taller than he first thought, the top of her head reaching up to his nose—a long meg with the most striking eyes he'd ever seen in his life.

They took in everything, were a deep, endless blue one could get lost looking into. He could vaguely remember her from her first Season, having heard of her when Redgrove had proposed. The day of the accident, he had seen her for the first time, bloodied and bruised.

He pushed the memory aside, wanting to remember her as she now was. Healthy and healed, as beautiful as any lady here and dancing with him.

He would make amends for the wrong he had done. Not that he would ever allow Miss Cooper to know of his hand in her injuries and loss of her betrothed, but he would make her world right. Make her future the one that she wanted, and he would move heaven and earth to gain her every wish.

She set her hand atop his shoulder, and he clasped her other. For the tall meg she was, her hands were small, delicate, and fit into his. He saw her take a calming breath, her grasp on his shoulder firmer than he was used to, but he supposed that was to help her dance with the injury she carried.

An injury he had a hand in causing.

"Tell me at once if you need to stop, Miss Cooper. I do not wish to dance if you are in pain."

Her eyes widened, but she let out a relieved breath. "You are very kind. I cannot thank you enough for your help."

"It is no trouble at all." The music started, and he swept her into the dance, surprised when she moved much better than one would think, considering she was lame at times.

Josh studied her with her so close in his arms. She should have little trouble in finding a match. The scar on her temple did little to take from her arresting features. Her striking eyes. Perfectly proportioned nose. She caught him ogling her and smiled, two delightful dimples forming on her cheeks.

He swallowed. Hard.

Dear God, Miss Cooper was a beautiful woman, and he was responsible for her. Well, his mother also, but he needed to find her a suitable husband. A caring and patient man. Save her from the rogues who would like to do nothing more than dally with such a beauty.

He cast his eyes about the room and noted several gentlemen watching them, contemplation in their eyes. He narrowed his eyes on Lord Templedon. The rake believed he could seduce any woman into his bed, and he was probably right, but not this one. Not the one who held on to him. Needed him.

"The duchess said that you too were looking for a wife this Season, Your Grace. I hope I'm not too forward in saying that I wish you well with your endeavors. May we both get all that we desire."

It was terribly forward of her, but then, she was from

Cornwall, and from what his mama had said of her favorite friend's daughter, had not been out and about in society much since leaving London all those years ago. One must make allowances.

He nodded. "I do hope that is the case, Miss Cooper."

She bit her lip, her eyes bright. "May I be so bold also to state you may call me Iris? Miss Cooper seems so droll. I know when we're in company that cannot be the case, but since you're going to be escorting me so very much, I think we shall both tire of Miss Cooper before I find a husband and are taken out of your care."

Josh tore his gaze from her lips, pinning his attention to the other dancers sweeping around them. "If you are certain, Miss Cooper, I'm more than happy to comply with your wishes and call you Iris."

He did not offer her the same ease of communication. After all, he was a duke, and he had a reputation and pedigree he needed to keep and adhere to. While he did not mind helping the handsome Iris, she was not suitable to be his bride, and his search needed continuing. If his potential bride found out he was on first-name terms with a woman living with his mama, he could lose his chance of happy matrimony before it even began.

"Thank you," she said, just as another couple crashed into them, causing Iris to stumble. He caught her before she tumbled to the ground. Her chest smacked hard up against his, and he stilled.

Not only was she tall, but she was all curves and lusciousness. Her hands clutched his nape, reminiscent of a pose he often took with the ladies he invited into his bed.

Josh set her back on her feet, reeling from the rioting reaction that sizzled to life inside him.

What on earth was wrong with him? He turned to the offending couple, glaring. "Take care, Stanhope."

He turned back to Iris and found her staring at him, something akin to a flush kissing her cheeks. He took pity on her, recognizing what she was feeling.

Desire. Shock. Awareness.

Everything he, too, now felt.

"A drink perhaps, Miss Cooper?" he asked, leading her from the floor.

She nodded, and he could not get them off the dance floor quick enough. The sooner he placed her back in his mother's care, the better.

One dance an evening, a little conversation, and that was all he would do.

For his own self-perseverance, if nothing else. Now she could be courted by those who did want her hand, and he had done his duty.

Just as he promised he would.

CHAPTER 5

The duke returned Iris to his mother after the dance, introducing her to several gentlemen who came over to write their names on her dance card. The scene reminded her of what her first Season had been like, full of possibilities and days and nights of balls and amusements that she had looked forward to attending.

Her life was different now. She was older, wiser, but also not so perfect as she had been. That gentlemen were standing before her, making pretty remarks went a long way in making her feel welcome once again. It was nice having flirty, light conversations. As much as she loved them, her parents were constantly asking her if she was well, did she need a tisane for the pain, more wood on the fire to warm the room, a pillow to help her comfort. Such conversations were tedious, and she was quite frankly sick of having them.

She had been injured in a carriage accident. It was time that she moved forward with her life. London, and the help of the duke and dowager duchess, would enable that.

A tall, light-haired gentleman joined their group. He picked up her gloved hand, bowing over it. He, too, was an attractive man, as tall as the duke, but where Penworth was dark and broody, this gentleman seemed light and amusing.

Opposites in all ways.

"Lord Templedon, may I introduce you to Miss Iris Cooper?"

"A pleasure," Lord Templedon murmured, his voice teasing. "Would you care to dance the next set with me, Miss Cooper? If you're not already engaged, of course." He slid a contemplative look to the duke.

"I am not engaged, my lord. I would like to dance," she replied, taking his arm.

His lordship led her out onto the floor, and she caught sight of the duke watching them. A shiver of awareness stole through her at the glower the duke's visage held. Did he not like Templedon? Iris looked up at the man placing them among the throng of dancers, wondering if something was wrong with him. Was he a rogue, a rake? Did he gamble?

"You're frowning at me, Miss Cooper. Do you find my company deplorable?"

She shook herself, laughing to cover her etiquette slip. "I apologize. I was woolgathering," she lied. "I'm very happy to dance with you."

He smiled, and she decided he could not be so very bad. Not when he had lovely, kind eyes such as he did.

"I'm glad to hear it. I understand you're from Cornwall. Is this your first Season?"

The question took her aback. The duchess had not schooled her on what to say should someone not know of her from her first Season.

"This is my second Season, my lord. I had my first several years ago, but it was cut short after a carriage accident."

"By ho, are you the miss who was thrown from the carriage in Hyde Park in '05? Killed old Redgrove, did it not?"

Iris felt her mouth gape. *Killed old Redgrove!* Had manners changed so much in the seven years she had not been in London that this was how one spoke? "Ah, yes, my lord. I was that unfortunate woman with Baron Redgrove when he lost his life."

The dance took her from his lordship for a moment, and she was glad of it. What sort of person spoke of such a tragic event as if it were some fodder for gossip? Did he have no empathy at all?

"I remember that year. Redgrove was a friend, you understand, not a close one, but we circulated in the same social sphere at times. I do not remember you, however, and I always remember a beautiful woman." His gaze traveled over her face, landing on her scar, and she fought the urge to explain it to him. To make an excuse as to why it was there.

Annoyance ate at her instead, and a little part of her wanted to make him uncomfortable by his ogling. His curt, unfeeling words. "I received this scar the same day Old Redgrove was killed. It is my trophy from that day."

Two pink marks formed on his cheeks, and for several turns of the dance, he could not look at her.

Iris was happy about the fact. She did not think they had much to say to each other, and certainly, she could never consider a man who spoke so dismissively of an accident that could happen to anyone as if it were nothing. Horses were flighty beasts at the best of times. In fact, Iris was surprised such accidents did not happen more often.

"Apologies, Miss Cooper. I did not mean to offend you."

She sniffed but refused to meet his eye. The dance came to an end, and even though there were two more dances within the set, she curtsied, wanting distance from him. "If you'll excuse me, my lord. I do believe I need to sit out the remainder of the set."

"Of course." He bowed, led her back to the duchess, and took his leave.

The duchess beamed with pleasure. "Templedon would be a good match, Iris. It is fortunate he has taken an interest. With his interest along with Penworth's help, you will have no trouble finding a husband."

Already the Season felt tedious, especially if gentlemen like Templedon made their interest known. She could never marry someone with no empathy and with little care for anyone else, except to gain enough fodder for gossip.

"I am not certain of Templedon. He seems a little unkind."

"Oh, my dear. Did he say something to offend you?" the duchess asked, reaching for her hand.

"A little, yes. I feel he does not have a compassionate heart. Too involved in himself to love another."

"Well, at least you know that now, dear. And the Season is young, and there are more gentlemen interested. Why look at them all, hovering close by, waiting for their turns to dance with you."

Iris studied them, all reasonably handsome, titled, and spoiled by their mothers and nannies. She could only hope there were some among them all who cared for others and did not speak so dismissively of people's tragedies.

Penworth certainly seemed to be such a gentleman, but then, he had shown no interest in her other than being affable and helpful. She was the daughter of a vicar. Even she was not fooled enough to reach so high as a duchess's coronet.

A pity, really, for Penworth was certainly handsome, eligible, and kind. He would make a good match for someone one day.

*J*osh led Iris and his mother into supper, deciding to sit with them and enjoy the varied and delicious feast the Cliffords had on offer. He was pleased with Iris's evening so far. The gentlemen had continued to present themselves, allowing him to introduce them, and she had danced with several of them. All but Templedon were a suitable match. They were all titled and wealthy, not looking to line their pockets with a dowry Miss Cooper did not have.

But there was something wrong with it all. Something that did not sit quite right with him. As much as he tried to support and care for his sisters, all of them were older than he was. And they had more than handled their journeys to their blissful married state. But Miss Cooper was different.

She needed protection, guidance, and support after all that had happened to her. He did not pity her, but it was certainly something that he could not name, a presence he felt whenever around her.

She sat across from him, laughing at his mother's recount of the night she had first met the duke, her future husband. Josh listened, smiling at the story, having heard it numerous times, how the duke had been set on marrying his mama's cousin, who did not want to marry him at all since she was already in love with someone else.

His mother had told the duke of her cousin's plight, and her strength and honesty had caught the duke's attention instead, and the rest, as they say, is history.

They were married not four weeks later.

Miss Cooper's eyes took on a dreamy state. Clearly, she adored the story as much as he always had, and it pleased him she did. He would ensure she found the same happy balance in her life. She was genuine, without guile or airs, and he liked that about her.

He liked it more than he ought.

CHAPTER 6

The following morning, Iris sat in the library, writing a letter to her mama, updating her on all her adventures so far. The shopping, the outings to the numerous balls and parties. That tonight they were to attend the opera at the Theater Royal, Drury Lane.

She had never attended the theater when she'd been in town during her first Season. Her mama having determined the outing too risqué for a debutante, so while her friends had attended, she had not.

But her mama was not here this time, and the duchess was, if anything, looking forward to the evening out more than Iris was herself.

"My dear, I have news," the duchess said, walking into the room and waving a missive in her hand along with a small printed card. "I have just received word that Lady Jersey, a patroness of Almacks, has bestowed on you a voucher for Wednesday next."

Iris placed down her quill, unable to quite believe what she was hearing. To gain entrance into Almacks was difficult, even if you were housed with a duchess, so exclusive were the assembly rooms. "That is good news. I was never admitted my first Season."'

The duchess frowned, coming into the room and ringing for tea. "They can be quite prohibitive of who they give admittance to, but as a granddaughter of an earl, you should have been invited."

Iris had not cared that she had not been invited. The patronesses of Almacks had always scared her a little. The women ruled London and could make or ruin a debutante's Season.

"I did not think I would be invited. Given the fact that I'm not overtly young and with my small limp, I would not have thought the patronesses would've liked that I was not perfect. When a title or wealth cannot gain one's entrance into Almacks, I stood little chance."

The duchess sat, her mouth pursed. "That is true. They can be narrow-minded, but we needn't worry about that now. You have an invitation, and we shall attend. Only respectable, reputable gentlemen will be in attendance. All of this shall help you in gaining the attention of a gentleman fit for your hand."

She nodded, but the idea of marrying gave her pause. Not that she did not want a husband, for she did, but a husband who loved her was above everything else that she required in a spouse. With no dowry, at least she would not have to worry about fortune hunters. Nor did she wish to marry a man who felt pity for her. Thought to give assistance and care every second of every day. That would never do.

She wanted a union that was equal in respect and love. She pursed her lips. Where did one find such a man and at her age?

The image of the Penworth floated through her mind, teasing her. So devastatingly handsome, kind, and willing to help when she required it. How lucky the lady would be, whoever caught his heart.

He would never look to her, and she wasn't fooled enough to allow herself to dream. A daughter to a vicar, no dowry and as far from perfection as one could be, did not make her equal to him.

"That is good news," Iris replied.

"Your silver embroidered gown will be delivered by next Wednesday, and you shall wear that. It is both stylish, elegant, and suitable for your age but not overpowering to the other debutantes who will be there."

Iris hoped she would not look like an old maid against the younger women vying for spouses. "My mama has given me leave to use her diamonds. Do you think they will suit the dress?"

The duchess clapped her hands, her smile bright. "They would do marvelously, my dear. You shall look beautiful."

A footman entered, carrying the tea tray, and Iris stood, joining the duchess on the settee. She poured the tea, handing a cup to Her Grace. "We have been to several balls already, but there have been no callers. Do you think my limp is keeping them away? I have tried to conceal it as much as I can when in public, but sometimes my leg becomes sore, and I cannot help how I walk." It was a concern that had been plaguing her for days. While others who lived on Hanover Square had multiple carriages roll to a stop before their doors, Duke Penworth's London home did not have any.

"We do not want any gentleman to call if they are not worthy or serious about their courtship of you. When we have a visitor, I'm sure he will be worth waiting for."

"Good morning, ladies," the duke said at that very moment, entering the room.

The duchess stared at her son with something akin to amusement. Iris did not mention the irony of His Grace turning up just after the duchess's declaration. She drank in the sight of him, wondering when she had become such an enthusiast of His Grace's presence.

He wore tan-colored skin breeches and Hessian boots splattered with mud. Had he come from the park, had he been out about town and was now only returning home? Not that this was where he was staying, he had his own lodgings, but the townhouse was where his office was located that dealt with all estate matters.

Or so he had stated.

He came and sank onto a high-back chair, leaning forward and pouring himself a cup of tea. She noted his cravat was loose, barely tied as it should be. In fact, taking in his appearance, she noted he looked somewhat ruffled. Whatever had he been up to?

From what she remembered of His Grace and the gentlemen he once ran about London with, it was probably not the sort of information she should be privy to.

Even so, her mind would not stop its train of thought. Was he out at his club? Or some hell in the East End? Did he have a mistress?

Iris sipped her tea, welcoming the calming brew that helped ease her mind with that worrying thought.

She was, she reminded herself, not worrying for her own interests but those of other young ladies whom he could court and eventually marry.

"Wonderful news, Josh darling. Lady Jersey has sent us a voucher for Iris to attend Almacks."

The duke raised his brow. "Well, that is good news. I shall try to attend with you both."

The duchess waved his offer away. "There will be no need for you to accompany us to Almacks, my dear. The patronesses, as you well know, only allow the highest echelons of society to attend. I'm sure my chaperonage will be enough for Iris."

The duke met her eye, and the pit of Iris's stomach fluttered. She sipped her tea, unsure why she was reacting to him in such a way. She supposed it was after their waltz that her mind had run away with her over how perfectly suitable he was for a husband.

She already knew he was kind, and he was wealthy enough not to mind her lack of funds.

What a pity you are so damaged.

Iris frowned into her tea, determined to ignore her cruel mind's taunt.

"Would you like me to escort you, Miss Cooper? I do not mind attending if it would help you in your quest to find a husband."

She shook her head, disappointment swirling through her at his words. Of course, he would not be looking at her as a potential prospect as a wife, and she was a silly fool to hope otherwise. To him, she was his responsibility, a lady to have married off, so his duty was complete.

How irritating.

"Thank you, but it is not necessary. I think Her Grace and I will be more than capable of maneuvering about Almacks for one night."

He smiled, and she hoped it was not relief she saw flicker in his blue orbs. "I understand you're to attend the theater this evening. I shall see you there also. The family box will be at your disposal."

Iris lost her breath at the idea of sitting in the ducal box. How wonderful. It made the prospect of this evening even more exciting.

"Very good. I was hoping you would notify the theater. I do hope they have stocked the box with my favorite flowers. The smells that sometimes waft up from the pit below are beyond endurable," the duchess said.

Iris had not thought about the body odor at the theater, but then, not everyone was as privileged as the Penworth family, and she supposed it was only probable that others would not bathe as often.

"I have, Mama," the duke murmured, his voice bored. "Just as I always do. No need to remind me."

The duchess's lips thinned into a displeased line. "One must check to ensure a pleasant evening. Now, we must leave you, my dear, and start preparing for this evening."

The duke caught Iris's eye, a small smile on his lips. "I shall see you this evening, Miss Cooper."

Iris followed the duchess from the room. What was the meaning behind the odd little looks that the duke kept giving her? Or was it only in her imagination that she was seeing them at all?

She hoped that was not the case. To have the duke interested in her would be a coup, but she could not let herself think such fanciful things. To do so would only lead to disappointment, and she had enough of that emotion in her life.

Tonight she would enjoy the opera, breathe the sweet-smelling flowers abundant in the ducal box, and ignore the fact that one of London's most eligible dukes sat beside her.

She sighed, following the duchess up the stairs. Easier said than done.

CHAPTER 7

*J*osh sat at Whites in his private room. *The Times* open on his lap, the first few lines of the story before him read numerous times as he thought of Miss Iris Cooper ensconced at his townhouse, making his mother more than adequately happy and busy with the Season.

He, too, ought to be increasing his search for a wife, but each time he attended a ball, picnic, or musical night all the women he had crossed paths with had done little to spark his interest.

He mulled over that quandary for a moment. Was he too severe in his expectations? His requiring only the most educated, titled, and wealthy woman to be his wife may make her difficult to discover.

A knock sounded on his door, and he bid them enter. He stood when he found the familiar and welcome visage of his brother-in-law. "Moore," he said, standing. "Come in, my good fellow. It is good to see you again."

"And you," the duke said, sitting across from him. A footman entered with another glass of brandy, taking

Moore's order and leaving again. "Isolde is busy with your mama and her new charge. I did not know the duchess was sponsoring anyone this year."

"Neither did I, until she shared the information." His mother was, if anything, a woman who knew her own mind and usually got what she wanted. "Miss Iris Cooper, but I'm sure Mama introduced you."

The duke settled himself in his chair, nodding. "We were, yes. She's very beautiful and sweet-natured. Isolde seemed to adore her instantly."

Josh raised his brows, surprised. "Isolde can sometimes be difficult to win over. I'm happy that Miss Cooper has prevailed. I assumed your being at Whites means you're here for the Season?"

"Isolde wished to attend, and I'm looking to purchase a new town carriage. I'm here to order one before we return to Wiltshire."

Moore's words reminded him that his curricle required replacing. He would do that before the end of the Season. "If you do not mind, I think I shall go with you when you order the new vehicle. My curricle has seen too many years and needs renewing."

"Of course." The footman returned, placing a beer before Moore before bowing and leaving them again. "Talking of carriages, and correct me if I'm wrong, but wasn't Miss Cooper injured in an accident several years ago? We attended the McCalter ball last evening, and her ladyship mentioned it."

"It is, unfortunately, true, and could be laid directly at my door."

Moore glanced up at his words, confusion clouding his gaze. "Whatever do you mean? How could such an accident be your fault?" he asked him.

Josh rubbed a hand over his jaw, glad to speak of his

concerns to a gentleman he could trust with his life. The knowledge and constant reminder of Miss Cooper's disability, her injury caused by his youthful foolery, plagued him daily, and he needed to speak of it. Release it into the world and seek penance, if only from a friend.

"The young Baron Redgrove wished to be part of our set. Desperately so. While we never denied or asked gentlemen new to town to associate with us, Redgrove was desperate to be one of our set. Somehow, it went around London that one must perform a risky maneuver for one to enter into our friendship group. Redgrove was determined to succeed, even though we never stopped him from joining us." Josh laid his head against the leather chair, wishing he could take back time, stop what had happened to Redgrove and Iris.

Damn his teasing, his testing of the young buck, all for a lark that went horribly wrong.

"I placed a bet in the book downstairs, stating that anyone who could circle Hyde Park the fastest in a phaeton would be a lifelong member. Redgrove took the bet, and one afternoon while Miss Cooper, his betrothed, was accompanying him, he thought to test his newly purchased phaeton's speed. It rolled, of course, killing him, and Miss Cooper was injured. When well enough, she left London several weeks later and has not returned until now."

Moore stared at him for several moments, and he hoped he did not see judgment, disappointment in his friend's visage, but even he knew it was there. In the shadows, whispered but never said aloud. Not to his face, at least. Perhaps it ought to be. He deserved no less.

"I killed Redgrove and maimed Miss Cooper for life. Mother does not know, and I would like to keep it that way."

"And Miss Cooper, does she not know what part you played in the bet? Even though I do think you take too much upon yourself. A silly bet in the book downstairs is not taken seriously. Everyone knows that. Redgrove was a fool to have tried such a caper. With Miss Cooper at his side at the same time, he was fortunate that she did not die along with him."

Josh stood, walking to the window and looking down on St. James street. The London populace out and about on this sun-shining day, shopping and socializing. He watched three children fleece a gentleman of his wallet, the man unaware of the street urchins' quick fingers. They darted back into a nearby alley, disappearing like shadows.

"She was severely injured and cannot remember much of that day at all. At this time, she does not know my involvement, and nor will she if I can keep that from her."

"And your plan for the Season now that she's under your family's care?" Moore asked him, sipping his beer.

"I will ensure she has a much happier ending to her Season than her last. This time she will marry a man who loves her as much as she loves him. It is my mission to make my wrong right by helping her, vetting all her gentlemen admirers to be sure she makes the right choice for her."

"Have there been many interested parties?"

Josh frowned, knowing there had not been. As to why though, he could not fathom. She was an earl's granddaughter. His mother, a duchess, was sponsoring her. There was no dowry, but she was not the only lady in town this year not to have one. Surely her injury was not so off-putting that the gentlemen kept away?

"No one has called, but the Season is young, and there are more events to attend. Tonight, in fact, I'm escorting Mother and Miss Cooper to the opera. I am hopeful that several callers will attend Mother's home tomorrow afternoon."

"We are attending the opera tonight. We shall join you in the Penworth box, show our support for Miss Cooper also. With us both at her side, she is sure to attract the correct sort of gentleman."

TAMARA GILL

"I do hope so. Her injury is not so bad that they should keep away." He had certainly not thought so. While it pained him to see her uncomfortable at times, she danced and enjoyed her time as much as any young lady. Her injury, if it was so very severe still, she had learned to hide well.

"She has an injury?" Moore queried. "Where?"

"You did not notice her slight limp? Her leg was fractured during the carriage accident. It pains her still."

Damn himself for playing with a gentleman who was not capable of thinking clearly. Who took bets without thought or care. If only he could turn back time, he would change so much.

"Hell, that is terrible for her, but surely that is not enough to keep men away. She is affable and handsome, which is what gentlemen of quality seek first in a woman. I know they are two traits most attractive to me."

That was true. His many friends had succumbed to a pretty face, not necessarily an heiress.

"I agree, of course, but I will evaluate interest and make adjustments where I can. I will not allow her to be a wall-flower. She must have suitors, admirers, and a proposal that makes her heart sing. I am determined to have it so."

"You are not to blame for her injury, Penworth. If the situation was explained to Miss Cooper, I'm certain she would say the same thing to you."

The idea of telling her the truth sent a cold shiver down his spine. He could not voice his wrongdoing, but he could change her fate, make amends to her life, and give her what she wanted.

A husband.

. . .

*I*ris stood in the foyer of the Duke of Penworth's London home and felt like the life she was leading was not her own. Her gown of mint-green silk with tulle that sat atop of it, so fine that it was almost transparent, did not feel real. The life she now led resembled more of a dream than reality.

She turned and caught a glimpse of herself in the mirror atop the hallstand, and she did not recognize the woman staring back at her. Where had the woman from Cornwall gone? The cripple who struggled whenever the weather turned chill. The young woman who pinned up her hair with little care whether it remained in place or not.

This evening the night was warm, and her leg hardly troubled her at all. She would make the most of her improvement, enjoy the opera and the ball that proceeded it. Dance until dawn.

Iris smiled at her musings, knowing that was probably not possible, but she would dance as much as she could, enjoy the flatteries the gentlemen made and see if any of them made an impression on her.

The duchess stood beside her, waiting patiently for her son to arrive to escort them for the evening. Although Iris knew His Grace would accompany them to the opera, she was not certain if he was attending the midnight ball.

How well and delicious that sounded. A midnight ball, where anything was possible, even for a woman such as herself. A little broken, but still perfectly fine for someone.

A footman moved and opened the door as if he sensed the duke's arrival. And how could one not sense the arrival of such a man? Her mouth dried at the sight of him. He was perfection itself, tall and handsome and utterly unattainable. Mayhap that was what made him so alluring. His Grace walked into the foyer, pulling his hat from his head, the easy lift to his lips in place making her inwardly sigh. He reached up to adjust his hair, and butterflies fluttered in her stomach. How she wished it was her hand running through his dark locks. Would he like her touching him so? Iris certainly knew she would enjoy petting him if she were able.

She still could not believe that she was here, living in this house with the Dowager Duchess Penworth escorting her about town. She would use the connection to her advantage, marry well and soon, so she was not a bother to them any more than she already was.

Not that the duchess would say such a thing. She was more than sweet and welcoming, but she was here for one Season only, and she needed to make the most of her time in London. Her injury plagued her, yes, but she needed to push through that pain, snap up a gentleman she could see herself married to for the rest of her life, and leave the duchess and duke to continue their lives without her.

He bowed before them, the scent of spice and apple renting the air. Iris breathed deep the alluring redolence. Was there nothing sweeter than a man who dressed well and smelled good enough to eat?

She dipped into a curtsy, grateful to bow her head so he would not see the heat on her cheeks at her wayward thoughts.

"Mother, Miss Cooper, how beautiful you both look this evening," the duke said, his gaze lingering on Iris a moment longer than appropriate before his attention moved over her like a caress right down to her silk-slippered shoes.

She adjusted her gloves, anything but to react to his appraisal.

"Shall we go, my dear? I do not wish to miss the beginning of the opera," the dowager said, moving toward the door.

The duke slapped his hat back on his head and held out

his arm as if remembering himself. "Miss Cooper, may I do you the honor?"

She took his arm, his coat as soft as velvet, more than happy to have the duke's arm. "Thank you, Your Grace," she said, looking toward the carriage outside, determined not to be distracted by the man beside her but the others who awaited, yet to be discovered.

CHAPTER 8

The opera was full, everyone eager to attend the Season's first performance featuring the famous Angelica Catalani. As the cast performed Mozart's *Le Nozze di Figaro*, the performance captured Iris under its magical spell. She appeared oblivious to everyone in the theater but the people on stage. Her eyes were bright and riveted to the performance, her bottom lip held tight between her straight teeth.

The image distracted Josh, and he doubted he had heard one second of the entertainment playing out before them.

The *ton* present who did not yet know of his mother's guest surveyed their box, curious about who the lady was and what she was doing with Penworth and his mother. They did not voice their curiosity, but their eyes certainly told a different story.

Josh watched those in attendance, strikingly aware that he had never had any lady sit within these curtained walls who were not his sisters over the past years.

He hoped the statement did not give the impression that Miss Cooper was a potential bride for himself, but he did live in the hope that other gentlemen would be curious as to who she was and make themselves known.

His sister Isolde sat beside him, her husband the duke to her right, who was engrossed in the performance just as Miss Cooper was.

Josh did not care a fig for the opera. He had heard it before. But the woman beside him had captured his attention from the first moment he had seen her this evening.

The vision of her had just about knocked his legs out from beneath him upon seeing her in the foyer of his home.

His breath had lodged in his lungs, and words for a moment or two were impossible to form. He knew she was pretty, but tonight it went beyond that benign word.

She was stunningly beautiful, an allure he had not expected to see blossom from her person. The gown of sheer silk gauze was distracting enough, but also the jewels that he knew were from his mother's private collection. The light-colored emerald that hung about her neck, dipping to the sweet crevice between her breasts, had captivated him. He had dipped into a bow to try to hide his interest, but it was no use. He could not stop admiring her person.

Tonight she looked like a duchess, and the realization gave him pause.

Blast it all to hell. She interested him. And she should not. Not at all. As beautiful as she was, she was neither titled, dowered, nor could she bring connections as lofty as his own.

He wanted a wife of beauty, intelligence, fortune, and breeding. And while Miss Cooper did have those in small articles, it was not enough. He was the Duke of Penworth. He had high standards to satisfy, especially after his parents, who had ruled London for several years.

He could not marry the penniless daughter of a vicar

from Cornwall, no matter how shiny she buffed to when dressed up.

You are such an ass, his mind rebelled, taunting him with the truth.

"Miss Cooper is delightful, is she not? When I first met her earlier today, I had no notion that a beautiful swan was hiding under all those ruffled feathers. Did you?" Isolde asked him, staring at him directly. His sister was never one to beat around the bush when she wanted to know something.

"She is most agreeable. I would think that a suiter will make himself known by tomorrow at home with Mother. Will you attend? Help me in choosing a suitable husband for our mother's sponsor. I do wish to make it right."

"Moore told me as to why. I hope you do not mind," she added, patting his hand that tapped on his knee. A tick he had not known he was doing. "I agree with Moore, what happened to Iris is not your fault, but I commend you on helping her, making right what you can. If this brings you peace, then I support you in that decision."

But did it bring him peace? Not really. Something told him he would forever feel guilty in the knowledge of his part of her accident. Until Miss Cooper knew the truth, how could he ever feel easy over the outcome she faced?

Even if he brought to her a most-sought-after gentleman, perfect for her kind heart, it would not change the fact she did not know the truth. She had not had the opportunity to decide who she thought deserved forgiveness or not.

"I will do what I can to make her future a little brighter than it was looking before she departed Cornwall."

"And you, brother. What of your future? I see Lady Sophie Hammilyn is here this evening. And if you have not noticed, she is quite taken with our box."

His sister inclined her head toward a box on the other side of the theater. Lady Sophie studied them without guile, her interest in their box obvious to any who noted it. "I spent some time last year at Lady Sophie's estate, and while she has been bestowed with beauty and a handsome dowry, she is a little curt and lacking in poise that I think is required in a duchess."

His sister chuckled but covered her slip with her hand. "Really, brother. Did she lack poise? Most of your sisters suffer from that very lack of tact as well. I did not think you would mind so very much that your wife would also."

It was not only poise. He clenched his jaw. "She could be quite cutting toward people too. While I do wish for my wife to have a strong constitution—God save her, she will need one being a duchess—I do not want her to be cruel to people less fortunate than she is. I feel Lady Sophie will do and say all that will gain her a ducal coronet, but not act so worthy of the title once the tiara is atop her head."

"Well, she seems quite determined. I would guess that she will visit our box this evening."

Josh cringed, hoping that wasn't the case. His interactions with the lady were awkward at best, especially since he was so keen when he first met her but was soon turned off when he gained a little insight into her personality.

"Victoria did not like her, to be blunt," he stated, not wanting to discuss Lady Sophie when he could continue admiring Miss Cooper. "In this case, I must agree with Victoria as to her feelings about the lady."

Isolde looked back at the stage, listening to the opera a moment. "I think Victoria would like Miss Cooper, just as I do."

He turned, studying his sister. What did she mean by that? Not that he did not know, he knew perfectly well that his sister was hinting at the fact that Miss Cooper would do very well as his duchess.

Josh ignored her and refused to reply to her statement.

He turned back to watch the performance and caught Miss Cooper leaning over to say something to his mama.

She had the loveliest neck, her profile accentuating her full lips. He swallowed.

Hard.

She was not for him. She was a family friend, a woman in need of support after her many trials. The last thing she required was a duke breathing down her neck, teasing her into a liaison that would go nowhere.

The idea of bedding her, of kissing her swan neck, of pulling down her mint gown and exposing her abundance of cleavage for his hungry lips made his cock stir.

He tore his gaze away, summoned a footman, and ordered champagne, anything to distract him from the diversion that was Miss Cooper at his side.

*I*ntermission came too soon, and within minutes of the break in the performance, the Penworth box was inundated with callers. All wishing the duke and his family a pleasant evening, asking what they thought of Angelica Catalani. Some of the ladies cast curious glances at Iris, but few took the time to speak to her.

Unfortunately, all her friends she had made her debut with were not in London this Season. She supposed they were married now, busy with their own lives and the many children they would have had—no need to attend London every year when one was so happily situated at their country estates.

A young woman entered the box with her father, making their way over to the duke without delay. She was all elegance and beauty and oozed confidence. Out the corner of her eye, Iris watched the woman's course, her fixation on the duke evident to not only herself.

"Lady Sophie, how lovely to see you again. Lord Hammi-lyn," the dowager duchess said. Lady Sophie dipped into a deep curtsy, demure and everything a good lady of breeding would do when before two ducal families.

"Your Graces," she said to both the duke and his sister. Her gaze moved across them all and stopped on Iris. The warmth she had felt in her gaze a moment before turned chill when her eyes settled on Iris.

Iris lifted her chin and waited for an introduction. A woman from Cornwall was strong of character. She would never look down to criticism, no matter how much Iris may wish to.

"This is my good friend's daughter, Miss Iris Cooper. She's staying with me this Season. Iris, this is Lady Sophie Hammilyn and her father, Earl Hammilyn," the dowager duchess said, introducing them.

Iris curtsied, thankful her hip did not protest the action after so much sitting. "It is very nice to meet you, Lord Hammilyn, Lady Sophie." She smiled, but the lady's fixed smile held little friendship. It seemed they were not destined to be friends. "How are you enjoying the opera so far? I must state that it has been a highlight of the Season so far," Iris said, trying to fill the void of silence.

Lady Sophie moved over toward her, taking her arm and pulling them a little away from everyone else. Iris went with her, unsure what was happening. "I enjoy it well enough, but it is nothing to a ball or musical evening with friends. Are you attending Lord McCalter's ball at midnight? There are to be fireworks, or so a friend of mine said earlier today at the modiste."

Iris smiled, unable not to at the thought of such enter-tainment. "We will be attending. I have never seen fireworks, but how marvelous I shall tonight."

"Hmm, yes, dear. And is the duke also accompanying you?" Lady Sophie asked, glancing over her shoulder.

Iris did also and found the duke watching them. "I am uncertain if His Grace is attending." Which was the truth. His Grace had not stated either way, to her at least.

Lady Sophie waved a footman over and took two glasses of Madeira, handing her one. "Well, no mind if he does not, you shall be there, and I'm certain we're to be great friends. Like you, I too am not the youngest debutante treading the boards this year. I spent several years in Spain living with my brother before returning home to do the pretty for my parents. They wish for me to marry, and so like you, I too am here to find a husband. But are they not the hardest objects to find?" she teased, laughing up at the duke who was now in conversation with Lord Hammilyn. "They do seem elusive. At least, I have had no luck so far, but the Season is young. I'm sure we shall both secure admirers at some point."

"I'm sure you are right," Iris agreed.

Lady Sophie sipped her Madeira, watching the duke over the rim of her glass. An uncomfortable, annoyed feeling settled in Iris's stomach at her fixation on the duke. Did Lady Sophie want the duke for herself? The thought of a union between them should not disassemble her so much, yet the churning in the pit of her stomach told her otherwise.

"Do you know the Worthingham's well?" Iris asked, her curiosity getting the better of her.

"We spent time together last year at my parents' home in Hampshire. I do not mind in telling you, since we are already friends, that I had thought the duke would propose. But he did state that he wished for me to have a Season. So, here I am, having a Season and waiting with bated breath as to when he may call."

So they were all but engaged!

Iris studied Lady Sophie, unable to believe such a tale.

The duke, from her limited knowledge of him, was honorable and kind. He would not lead any lady with the belief of a union. What was Lady Sophie trying to do by telling her such a story?

"I wish you well in your endeavors," she said, sipping her drink. "But surely the duke is not the only peer in London who has caught your attention. You're a beautiful woman. I'm sure many men are chasing you all over London."

Lady Sophie released a tinkling laugh, and ice shivered down her spine. What was it about this lady that she distrusted? She did not know her at all, yet she would guard her words and actions when around Lady Sophie. She did not want to make an enemy of her. That would be the worst outcome of her time in London. But nor would she be a close confidant either.

"There are, of course, but none of them are dukes." Lady Sophie grinned just as a footman announced the opera was about to restart. "I will see you at the ball, Miss Cooper. We shall continue our association there."

Iris nodded, a smile wedged on her lips, one even she could feel was not genuine. She hoped Lady Sophie could not tell. "I look forward to it," she called after her, not the least excited about the prospect.

CHAPTER 9

*T*he opera was everything that Iris wished it to be, and it was over before she realized it. They were one of the first to leave, the ducal carriage rolling up before Theater Royal, Drury Lane. The duke helped his mother before turning and taking her hand, helping her step into the vehicle.

Her gown caught beneath her shoe, and she slipped, but before her leg scraped down the carriage step, the duke was there, his strong, warm arms wrapped about her waist, stopping her downward trajectory.

Her body burned at his touch, his warm breath grazing her cheek. She steadied herself with her hands against his chest, her mind screeching to a halt at the chiseled, hardened muscles beneath her palms.

She breathed in his sweet apple scent, moving away as fast as she could before anyone noticed that she thoroughly enjoyed being rescued by His Grace, and before his mother!

Worse, however was now that she had touched him once, it would not be enough, that she would crave the feel of him from this night on.

Iris met the dowager's concerned gaze, releasing a shaky breath that the duchess had not noticed Iris's reaction to her son.

Not that she would ever dare wish for more from the man. He was not for her. He would marry a lady far above her status, if not wealth. A woman who struggled to walk on the coldest of days, who did look as if she had been in a tavern brawl, was not his intended. His wife would be perfect, unblemished from life—a diamond among paste.

She was not that lady.

"Are you injured, my dear? Do take care. The steps can become slippery with a little dust upon them."

"I am quite well," she assured the dowager, trying once again to enter the equipage without causing injury to herself or anyone else.

The duke followed them and sat across from her, his gaze fixed on the outdoors before he thumped the roof, and they were off. His attention moved from the passing shop fronts and homes that lined the London streets and collided with hers.

Iris's heart thumped hard in her chest. His dark, hooded gaze did not shift, and she had the oddest feeling he was contemplating something. Was he debating now joining them at the ball? She supposed now that he had seen Lady Sophie again mayhap that had changed his mind.

Iris dismissed the thought as soon as she had it. She did not want to think of Lady Sophie or any other lady for that matter, so long as he kept looking at her as he now did. Like a man overrun with concupiscence. With wants and needs that she may be able to meet.

Not that she knew anything about such emotions, but she had caught glimpses of such looks from her betrothed before he passed.

What those looks meant, however, with Penworth, she could not say. Possibly, he could not either.

She sighed, breaking eye contact, and studied her hands in her lap instead. It wasn't very reasonable of her to believe he would contemplate anything with her. He was looking out for her. Helping her navigate the Season now that she was having another after so long away from London.

There was nothing to his look other than companionable friendship.

"I will attend McCalter's midnight ball with you after all."

The dowager looked at her son, clearly surprised by this turn of events. "How lovely, my dear. But I feel I must warn you there will be ladies present who will wish to dance."

He shrugged, his attention once more on the passing city outside the carriage windows. "It is too early to return to my lodgings, and I have no other commitment. Moore said he would also be in attendance with Isolde. We shall make a merry group."

Iris could not agree more. How lovely for the Worthinghams to have such a close family. The five siblings certainly seemed fond of each other. As an only child, she had longed for a sibling, but alas, her mama had never borne one. That her mother was also an only child, cousins were but a dream too.

"Will any of your other sisters attend this year?" she asked, wanting to feel at ease after the odd looks from the duke only minutes before. Her stomach fluttered still, which would never do. She would not allow herself to dream, to hope for anything more with the duke. His family having already been more than welcoming and helpful.

"We may see Elizabeth, but Victoria and Alice will not be in town. When the Season draws to a close, I'm traveling back to Scotland to spend time with my eldest daughter, Elizabeth."

The duke made a scoffing sound, and Iris looked at him curiously.

"Do not scoff, Your Grace. You are friends with Muir. No need for any animosity."

Curiouser and curiouser. Whatever happened between them, she couldn't help but wonder.

The duke raised his brow, attempting to look down his nose at his mother, and failing miserably with the steely gaze his parent shot back at him. "That is debatable. Friends may be too broad a term."

"You do not like him because he defended himself when you flew at him with your fists." The duchess turned to Iris. "My son, you see, is a little overprotective of his sisters, and Elizabeth had been hurt by Muir years before their marriage. His Grace could not forgive as easily as Elizabeth."

"They are happily married now?" Iris asked, looking forward to the day she may meet the duke's sister, all of them in fact.

"Oh yes, for many years now. Muir is a Scottish earl."

"I would like to travel to Scotland, although I have heard it is terribly cold."

"Your husband may treat you, Miss Cooper. When you find him, you shall have to ensure it is part of the marriage contracts."

Iris nodded, pinning a smile to her lips at the duke's words. His statement filled her with disappointment. The idea that he had meant anything by his heated gazes was a silly notion she would not allow herself to have again. His statement had put paid to such fanciful thoughts. While she may wish for more, he certainly was not reflecting in that way.

The carriage rolled to a stop before the McCalter's townhouse. The home was lit like a beacon of light, shining brightest in the dim street. Carriages lined both sides of the road, and people were everywhere as they made their way toward the entrance.

They, too, stepped down from the carriage, making their way toward the house. Iris was jostled and separated from the duchess, who moved forward, unaware of what had happened. She came up to the door, and a footman stepped in front of her, halting her progress.

"Do you have an invitation? All guests must be accounted for," he stated, glancing at her hands that were empty.

"I'm here with the Dowager Duchess of Penworth and her son the duke." Iris pointed to the duchess, who was now speaking to the hostess, unaware that Iris was not at her side.

The footman raised one mocking brow. "Her Grace does not seem to be missing her companion. Please move aside, and make way for the other invited guests."

He looked past her, dismissing her. Iris gasped, heat burning her cheeks. She stepped aside, unsure what she should do next. Should she try to track down the carriage or find a Hackney cab and return home?

"Miss Cooper is with me." A deep baritone sounded behind her.

Penworth placed her hand on his arm and walked past the gaping footman without a by your leave. Iris glanced over her shoulder and could not help the small laugh that bubbled up and out.

"You're my hero, Your Grace. Thank you," she teased, smiling.

He smiled back, his blue eyes alight with amusement. "I loathe uppity servants as much as I loathe uppity aristocrats."

A warm, fuzzy feeling settled in her belly at his words. It was not every day a handsome duke saved a lady, and she would enjoy the moment for what it was. His Grace merely being a friend, a gentleman. Now she needed to find one of her own.

CHAPTER 10

"*How* ow dare the duke throw such a lady before me without care to my feelings. This is not right, Father, and you should make the duke do the right thing by me."

"Sophie, darling, the duke has made no promise to you. If every gentleman who called upon our estate in Hampshire was required to offer marriage, you would have been married as a babe."

Sophie sighed, rolling her eyes at her father's pathetic attempt to soothe her ire. She would not be soothed. She wanted the duke, and the poor little vestal virgin from Cornwall thought she would have the coronet. Well, she would not. The Penworth coronet would be hers to wear. It would be she who would give the duke children, a male heir, not some woman whom no one cared to remember after she left London seven years before.

"She was injured in a carriage accident, and I suppose it is very nice of the duke and his mother to help her gain a marriage, sponsor her, but she is impeding my ability to get close to the duke, and I will not have it."

"No," her father asked, raising a skeptical brow. "And how will you stop the duke from remaining by Miss Cooper's side? Tell him that you do not care for her and that he ought to be paying you more attention?"

Sophie growled, grinding her teeth. Her father really could be the most vexing man. "I do not know how I will make him come over to me, but I shall. I'm an heiress, an earl's daughter, a lady in my own right. I am perfect for him, and he will know it before the Season is over." And if he did not come to his senses, she would force him in some way or another.

"Sophie darling, you cannot make someone enamored of you. It must come naturally, or you will find your marriage to the duke, or whomever you choose based on rank and wealth, will not be a happy union."

"Pfft," she scoffed. "I do not care for emotions. I know what I want and what will make me happy, and the duke is what I desire above all else. I do not care if he does not love me, but we are a good match. It would be a welcome alliance between our great families."

Earl Hammilyn sighed, staring out at the London streets. "Do not regret your choice, my child. Marriage is a lifelong commitment and one you will wish you had right from the moment you say I do."

"Father. I do not understand this romantic notion of yours."

"I do not understand your lack of one."

Sophie shrugged, checking her gloves and dress before they arrived at the McCalter's midnight ball. The duke would be hers, and if she had to befriend the little Cornwall chit to be near him, show him it was she he wanted and no one else, then she would do so. No one cut her out of what she wanted, and those who got in her way would be dealt with,

Miss Cooper not excluded. She narrowed her eyes, taking a calming breath.

One would not think the ball would be as energetic along with a crush at the late hour that they attended, and yet, one could hardly move around the room, less carry on a conversation without yelling at the top of one's voice.

Josh stood near the smoking room doors, having found his brother-in-law Moore absent from his wife, an unusual occurrence and a situation one should always take the opportunity to enjoy.

He studied the room, sipping a whisky, and watched as a horde of men started to parade before Miss Cooper, at first assessing her like some prize before going up and requesting his mother introduce them.

Josh supposed he should be there, doing the honor, but it was probably best that he was not. A duke hovering close by could put some gentlemen off, and he wanted Miss Cooper to make a match. To find someone to whom she could see herself married for the rest of her days.

That this evening she looked utterly stunning helped also. There was no sign of her injured leg, and the scar on her temple was not so very bad.

Her large, blue eyes were filled with pleasure and amusement as more and more gentlemen joined them, her laughter reaching across the room to tease his senses.

"Miss Cooper is a beauty this evening. I think she has finally been seen," Moore stated. His friend's gaze fixed on the lady as much as Josh's was.

"I'm happy for her." And he was happy, even if the sight of all the gentlemen vying for her hand left an odd, uncomfortable feeling lodged in his chest. Would they be kind to her?

Were they gamblers who would leave her destitute when they had run through all their funds? Did they know of her injury and would be considerate of it?

"I would not allow Templedon near her. I heard he has pockets to let after a disastrous night at one of the hells in East London. It is rumored that he's at risk of losing his estate."

Josh's pleasure dissipated at the sight of Templedon bowing over her hand and being forward enough to brush his lips against her gloved fingers.

The rogue.

"I will speak with him should he call, find out the truth. I will not allow her to be taken in by such a false emotional ruse."

"You may also need to look into Lord Daniel's finances. He has some outstanding IOUs that he is avoiding paying. He is known for being tight when it comes to his blunt. He may be merely being mean, or he too could be in financial strife."

Josh clapped his brother-in-law on the back, glad for the information. Just then, he caught sight of Miss Cooper being led out onto the floor by Lord Templedon. His jaw clenched, not particularly relishing the sight of the man with Miss Cooper on his arm.

He was a smug bastard. Too aware of his wiles when it came to women.

Moore chuckled beside him. "Now, now, Penworth. No glowering at the guests. You're assisting Miss Cooper, not attempting to scare away all her suitors."

Josh schooled his features, unaware that he was so public with his reaction to seeing her being led out by a man he knew was unsuitable. She was an earl's granddaughter, a vicar's daughter, she may not be overly high on the social ladder, but she deserved better than a husband who would continue to whore his way around Covent Gardens any chance he gained.

"I should put a stop to the dance, should I not?" he suggested to Moore, narrowing his eyes at his sister's husband when he grinned.

"If you want everyone here to know that you are vying for her hand and not merely acting as a guardian of sorts. I would let things play out this evening, keep your distance and see if any gentlemen call on her or yourself in the coming days. You can make your feelings known at Penworth house better than in McCalter's ballroom."

"Yes, you are right. I shall refrain." But the longer the night went on, the number of gentlemen asking for Miss Cooper's hand to dance was bordering on the absurd.

She did not have one dance spare before supper at the ungodly hour of two in the morning took place. He escorted his mother and Miss Cooper to the supper room and did not miss her relief as she sat across from him. Nor did he miss her flushed skin. Her chest rose and fell rapidly from all the dancing. He swallowed, unable to remove the vision from his mind of her ample bosom.

The little mole that sat directly between both breasts. Dear God, had that mole been there the entire time?

He licked his lips, wondering what she would taste like. As sweet as she smelled, of roses, jasmine and lavender and everything delightful. Her smile as she talked to his mother was full, honest, and utterly charming.

How had he not seen that she was such a treasure? How had the other gentlemen not have seen either?

Were they all blind?

He glanced about the supper room, many eyes upon them, men with admiration, curiosity, and interest, women with annoyance and disdain.

Lady Sophie Hammilyn one of them, watching them play

at their table as if they were all sport. He no longer thought of the possibility of them, not after his time with her in Hampshire. As well-bred as she was, or how refined, she would never be his duchess.

"I'm going to go for a ride tomorrow in the park. Would you like to accompany me, Miss Cooper? Mother can ride alongside us in the carriage to ensure you're suitably chaperoned."

Her eyes widened with pleasure. "I would like to, yes. If your mama says she will accompany us."

His mother bit into her millefruit biscuit, and it took her several moments before she replied, "Of course, I shall accompany you."

"I think Daisy will suit Miss Cooper. She is calm and tame around traffic," he stated, wanting to put Miss Cooper at ease over the mount she would ride.

"You are always so thoughtful and protective, my dear."

Josh ignored his mother's words, unsure if she meant kindly by them or was pointing out his overprotective nature. Iris's accident had been his fault, and fear had spiked within him of causing another, of not being a good brother, keeping his sisters safe from harm, be that of the male kind, or some other type of accident.

He may have been too protective at times, but at least they were all safe and happily married now. He would do the same for Miss Cooper. "Do you have any dances left on your dance card this evening?" he asked her, sipping the claret and wishing he'd taken a glass of brandy instead of the dry red beverage.

"I have one left, a waltz." Miss Cooper lifted up the little card hanging off her wrist, reading it as if to ensure she was correct. "All the others are taken."

"How popular you are this evening, my dear," his mother

remarked. "Is it the gown? It suits you, and you look simply lovely."

"Or it could be that the gentlemen have finally noticed your beauty, inside and out." His mother's gasp brought his to attention to what he had just said.

Aloud.

Miss Cooper grinned into her dessert, his mother looking at him as if he had lost his mind. Which, when he was around Miss Cooper, had been occurring more and more.

What possessed him to say such things to her? He was not courting her, even if she looked so very fetching right now, all flushed and abashed.

"May I request the waltz, Miss Cooper?" he asked, ignorance over what he had said the best course of action. He should not be taking up a valuable dance that she could be enjoying with a gentleman who did wish for her to be his wife.

He was not that man. Nor could he stop himself.

She peered at him, mulling over his words, and for a dreadful moment, he thought she might refuse until her lips lifted into a sensual smile that left his wits scattering.

Who knew Miss Cooper could be so alluring?

He did a mental calculation of how much spirits and wine he'd downed this evening, to be sure he wasn't in his cups.

"You may," she answered him finally.

Josh could not look away from her, even as his mother watched on with something akin to shock. Up until the waltz, he would make a point of dancing with others. He did not need the *ton* wagging their gossiping tongues over who he was courting or considering for his duchess.

That would end such rumors and leave him free to court whom he did wish to be his wife.

Which right at this moment, he had no fucking clue whom to choose.

CHAPTER 11

*T*he few sets that Iris had danced earlier in the night were soon forgotten at the delicious expectation of dancing with His Grace. A waltz, no less.

Penworth.

London's most eligible bachelor this Season and in search of a wife. Iris would dance and enjoy being in the man's arms for as long as she could before he belonged to someone else's heart.

He led her out onto the floor. His superfine coat was soft against her palm, and she hoped he could not sense her racing heart. Her body did not feel her own when she was about him. A feeling she could not remember when with Dudley. At no point had the duke made his attentions toward her anything but benign friendship, and so she was at a loss as to why she felt this way. Her reactions were not warranted nor helpful, not if she was going to marry someone else.

When she found the right gentleman for her, that was.

The duke swooped her into the waltz, his hand high on her back. A shiver stole through her at his nearness, his warmth and scent, everything she'd come to appreciate more than was proper.

Iris looked up, wanting to admire his handsome visage, and found him staring at her. His eyes blazed with an emotion she could not interpret. Her breath caught, her heart raced, and there was no place she would rather be than in his arms.

"Have you found anyone who has sparked the interest of your heart?" he asked her, his voice light but serious.

Iris wished she had her wits about her like he still did. Her attention snapped to his lips as they moved. He had lovely lips, full and wide, perfect for kissing. Oh, to dream of being in his arms and the lucky lady he kissed. Something told Iris he would be passionate, caring, and satisfying beyond measure.

Iris schooled her features, forcing herself to stop thinking about the duke in such a way. "There are two gentlemen whom I enjoyed the company of. A Mr. Reeves and Lord Bradley. What are your thoughts on their eligibility?" she asked him. After all, acting as a type of guardian for her, the duke was looking into anyone who made their suit known and letting her know the particulars of their desirability.

Talking of her prospective suiters was a safe conversational subject. For her, at least, she felt nothing but benign friendship toward all of the men she had met so far.

Penworth she had to exclude from the innocuous list.

A muscle flexed in his jaw, and his hand tightened about her waist, pulling her the sparsest closer to him. The breath in her lungs hitched. He was too close for clear thought. His mere presence made her mind befuddled and dizzy, as if she'd imbibed too much wine.

"Bradley is a rake. Not for you." His answer curt and blunt. "Mr. Reeves I will consider further and let you know the outcome of my investigations."

"Thank you," she said, happy to wait for as long as the duke wished. The longer he took in picking out a suitable husband, the longer she would have with him and his mama. If only he would look at her for his prospective bride. Iris was certain she could make him happy and give him children. Her injuries, the doctor had stated, would not stop her from such a future.

"You do not like Bradley. I fear he will be quite disappointed," she said with a touch of pity. "I do believe his suit is in earnest," she teased, hoping her insight into the duke's reaction to the man's name was not wrong.

"I'm sure it is," His Grace spat, shaking his head. "He's after a biddable wife, not a love match. He will not do for you."

She grinned, pleased the duke wanted love for her and not just a suitable match who pleased both families. "He's very handsome. I do find myself quite enraptured by his cheekbones. Marriage to him would not be so very bad."

The duke gaped, and Iris wondered if she'd been a little too forward, even with a man who had no romantic interest in her whatsoever. "I apologize," she added quickly, not wanting him to think her fast. "I do speak plainly with people I consider my friends. I hope you are not disappointed in me, Your Grace."

He spun her near the turn of the room, her chest brushing his silk waistcoat. Heat pooled between her legs. She could not keep reacting to Penworth in this way. It would only lead to heartache, hers in particular.

His dark, troubled gaze met hers. Iris swallowed, the sense that she was getting in over her head with the duke floating through her mind.

"We are friends, and I will guide you as best I can, but the choice of who you will marry will be yours and no one else's. If you want to marry Bradley, while I would warn you against such choice, I would not stop you from making it."

"You do not mind me speaking my mind, Your Grace? My father is forever telling me to stop being so opinionated, at least in the presence of others."

"I'm used to independence and forward-speaking women. I have four sisters, remember?"

She chuckled, looking forward to meeting them all one day. If that day ever happened. Her mama and the duchess were friends, and now that Iris knew the dowager duchess so well, surely they would connect more in the future.

She hoped that was the case.

You would have to see the duke and his new wife if that were to occur.

Iris threw the thought aside. Seeing the duke married would be no issue. Had she started a love affair with him, had he been courting her and then chose another, she may find such a situation hard, but he was not. He was her friend. She would be happy for him and nothing more.

"I want to tell you that Redgrove's mother wishes to have tea with me next week. An invitation arrived this morning."

He watched her as they continued to weave about the floor. "You are nervous about seeing her again? Is that why you are telling me?" he asked her.

She sighed, biting her lip. She was nervous about it. They had not held out the hand of friendship since Dudley's death, and it seemed odd that she would do so now. "I did not think they liked me. I'm confused why Lady Redgrove would request an audience."

Penworth cleared his throat, staring off over her shoulder. "Redgrove was a cheerful fellow, always willing to please." He threw her a quick smile. "I'm sure her ladyship is no different and merely wishes to repair your friendship with her family."

That was certainly true. Dudley was cheerful and forever up for a lark. The race around Hyde Park, unfortunately, his last. "You are right, of course. Lady Redgrove would never chastise me now over an accident that was not my fault." Iris sighed, thinking back to her time in London before the disaster. "I wish I could remember the day, but no matter how much I try, I cannot. Lord Templedon even mentioned that he knew Redgrove and remembered me, but I could not remember him."

The duke frowned and appeared more displeased than she'd ever seen him before. "Templedon should not have brought up a subject that is still so obviously painful for you. It was inconsiderate of him."

"It is no longer painful. Merely sad that Dudley lost his life over something so foolish. I'm sure were he still alive today, he would even state the same."

"*J*'m sure he would," Josh answered, his mind whirling at what Miss Cooper had said. Templedon used to be part of his set, and he was well aware of what had occurred leading up to Redgrove's death. The bet, that they had all congregated at Hyde Park to see if the baron could beat a previous time set by Josh.

Was he planning on using what he knew about that awful day to make Miss Cooper marry him? He caught sight of the gentleman in question. His smirk smacked into him like a physical blow. Would he demand Josh allow Miss Cooper to marry him to keep his mouth shut over Josh's involvement with the carriage accident? She was not an heiress or titled. What did Templedon want with her?

Same as you do. A wife of poise and grace who would be an asset to any family she married into.

"Be on your guard with Templedon. I'm uncertain

whether he is trustworthy, and to be as honest with you as I can, his lordship is rumored to be ruined financially. I do not want to see you saddled with a husband who will leave you destitute. Templedon only came into the title two years past. The late earl was wealthy, and yet, it looks as if the coffers are now empty."

Miss Cooper's tongue darted out to dampen her lip. Josh felt the action right down to his core. He breathed deep, wanting to close the space between them and kiss those ample lips. Thrust his tongue against hers, make her moan his name against his ear at the peak of her release.

His cock stirred, and he separated them a bit, not wanting to see her run off, terrified of his reactions to her presence.

"I will do whatever you suggest, Your Grace. I do not want a union that leaves me disillusioned and alone, penniless as well."

"I would not allow that to happen to you. I'm here to protect and guide you. I shall not let you down." Not again, at least. He had let the woman down in his arms once before, with terrible repercussions for his actions. His attention took in the scar she bore on her face, a small red line that ran from her temple to her forehead—hardly anything, but in turn, everything. The line was a reminder of all he'd done wrong, of what she had endured at his urging and foolishness.

She tipped her head to the side, studying him. "I do think you take too much responsibility on, Your Grace. When it comes to me, at least. I do not deserve such kindness, not from you. It was the dowager duchess who sponsored me, agreed to guide and care for me while I'm in London. I do not want to take up too much of your time, not when you have a Season to attend to as well. I feel as though I am monopolizing your time."

She turned her head and stared to the side of the room. Josh followed her line of sight and caught notice of Lady

Sophie watching them, her mouth pulled tight into a displeased line.

"I would prefer you take up my time than any others who look to further their standing by an advantageous match. If my mother is sponsoring you, then you are a woman of morals and good judgment. I do not fear your company."

Her eyes took on a dreamy hue. "How lovely you are."

He let out a bark of laugher, unsure if she meant to be so honest. The rosy hue kissing her cheeks told him she had not meant to be. "Why, thank you, Miss Cooper. So are you." He spun her quickly, wanting to make her at ease. "You have done remarkably well tonight. I hope your leg will not pain you on the morrow."

"Oh, it will." She shrugged as if it were a matter of fact. "But I no longer care. This evening, the opera, the ball, this waltz has been too enjoyable to regret."

Her words warmed his heart and made his blood quicken. He enjoyed her in his arms too. Much more than he thought he would. She was a vicar's daughter. A woman beneath his notice, until now.

Now, he'd seen her. Witnessed how sweet-natured and pure she was, how kind and generous and utterly one of the most handsome women he had ever met in his life.

A woman who sparked to life a fire inside him that he was unsure he could keep within controlled lines. Something told him eventually the fire she stoked would run out of control, and, scariest truth of all, he wouldn't do anything to try to stop it.

CHAPTER 12

The following afternoon they rode down to Hyde Park, his mother ensconced in the open carriage and moving ahead of them in the traffic. Iris had not been on a horse in several months, but the mare, Daisy, whom the duke had picked out for her, was placid and not at all perturbed by busy London traffic.

The duke kept a close vigil of her horse, always within reach of the reins, always protective and caring. Iris surreptitiously studied him. What had made him so shielding of others? He said himself he may have overstepped the bounds of keeping his sisters safe during their Seasons. Away from gentlemen admirers even, but likewise with her, he seemed to be going out of his way to accommodate Iris.

A small part of her could not help but hope it was because he enjoyed her company. May even be considering her as a potential bride. More likely, he was caring for her as if she were like a sister of his.

The idea left a sour taste in her mouth. She did not want the duke to see her in a familial kind of way. She certainly did not look upon him with innocuous eyes.

Whenever she was around him, like at this very moment, all she could think about was his sweet nature. How handsome and dashing he was. How women glanced his way from the park's walkways, their eyes sparkling with interest and pleasure. Men tipped their hats toward one of the highest members of the *ton*, hoping for an introduction.

The duke rode a little ahead of her, his shoulders broad and strong, his hands capable on the reins. He kept vigil, kept her safe, and she could not remember the last time she had felt so well cared for.

Not that her parents did not care for and love her, for they did, but the duke and the dowager duchess, too, were not family. They did not have to go out of their way to be there for her, yet they were.

She would forever adore them both for their kindness.

He glanced over his shoulder, his dark-blue gaze hit her like a physical blow. The breath in her lungs stilled, her nipples prickling under her riding gown, and she was thankful for the thick riding jacket she wore.

"We are almost there, Miss Cooper," he said, his lips twisting into a knowing grin.

How she wanted to kiss those lips. Last evening, after the sweetest waltz she was certain ever to entertain, she had dreamed of him. Of them, more to the point. Alone and dancing in his London lodgings off Piccadilly.

The dance had started innocently enough until the duke had closed the space between them, no longer satisfied with merely dancing.

Iris bit her lip, remembering the dream. His large hands, slipping down her body, slowly working her dress up and over her person.

He'd kissed her then. His lips as soft as she imagined them, his mouth hungry and demanding her surrender.

She had, of course. In fact, she had not woken from the

dream until the duke had laid her upon a settee and pushed against her wet, aching core.

Iris had woken in a pool of sweat, her breaths short and quick. For hours she had lain there, remembering every moment of her dream, reliving it, wanting it to be true.

And that was the crux of her problem being here in London and staying with the duke's mama.

She wanted him. Not only as a friend but a lover. A husband.

"Do you think there will be many at the park today?" she asked, a little trepidation running through her as the gates to the park rose up before them.

A memory twitched at the back of her mind, of riding through those very gates in a highly sprung carriage. Of laughter and chatter before it all went so wrong.

She could not remember the accident, but the gates were familiar and brought back a memory she had long thought lost.

Did that mean she could remember more?

Did she even want to? The vision would not be kind.

"I should think so. The Season is well underway now, but do not worry. I shall keep you safe, and should you require to return home in the carriage, the dowager duchess will oblige, of course."

"Of course." Not that she would be returning in the carriage. She was determined to spend the hour or so at the park beside the duke. Her unattainable dream to be his may never come true, but she would enjoy his company while she could.

They rode into the park, following the dowager's carriage. The duke dipped his head to several passers-by, and Iris greeted them when they included her in their salutations.

"I see Mr. Reeves is here and riding our way. I think I shall have to share your company for our excursion."

Iris looked out onto the park grounds and did indeed spot Mr. Reeves trotting over in their direction. She inwardly sighed, not wanting to share her time with the duke with anyone else.

But she could not think that way. The duke would never marry her, whereas she could have a secure and happy life with the wealthy landowner from Kent. He seemed a happy, sweet man, willing to do whatever she asked. There was no reason why he would change his ways after they were married.

"Mr. Reeves," she said when he arrived, his smile wide, his eyes bright with pleasure. If only she felt the same way for the gentleman. Looking at him, she did not feel anything for him, no matter how much easier her life would be if she did. "How lovely to see you at the park today."

"It is I who is satisfied, Miss Cooper." He moved his horse about hers and came to ride alongside. The duke moved ahead, giving them privacy.

"I did not think you could ride a horse. I had heard that after your carriage accident, riding a horse was impossible."

For a moment, Iris could not reply. She wracked her mind to consider who could state such a thing about her. Certainly, she had not expressed such a fact. "I can ride sidesaddle without ailing, Mr. Reeves, if that is what you wanted to know." She adjusted her seat, looking ahead. "I would be appreciative to know who said such a falsehood."

Her words were curter than they ought to be, but what gentleman stated such a thing and to a woman too, without finding out first if it were true? Surely such manners had not changed since she had been in society last.

"I'm pleased to see that I have been misinformed. As for who told me, I could not say. I may have even heard it in passing during a ball."

Iris took a calming breath, taking a moment or two to

ignore the fact people were talking about her injury and making her out to be a cripple.

The duchess stopped ahead of them to speak to Lady Leslie, who was passing in another equipage. The duke halted, and Iris did the same. Mr. Reeves, however, did not seem to be taking notice that the carriage ahead had stopped. He continued to ride along, his nose high in the air as if he were still accompanying the duke and herself.

"I think Mr. Reeves may not be as intelligent as I first thought him. I do not believe he will be suitable for a woman such as yourself, Miss Cooper."

She raised her brow, believing that herself. "Really? Why do you say, Your Grace?" she asked him, curious to know his reasons.

His eyes captured hers, and she was powerless to look away. Did not want to if she were honest with herself. "Because I could never give you away to a fool."

There was something in his voice, his eyes that promised he would not give her away to just anyone. But it was not only that. His eyes burned with heat, a longing she was starting to relate to. Did the duke want to kiss her as much as she wanted to kiss him? Did he want to touch her as much as she wanted to touch him?

How she wished she were brave enough to ask. But she was not. The daughter of a vicar did not ask men to kiss her. They married and had babies, did their duty for their family and what society expected of them.

Something told Iris that such a life would never satisfy her. Not after being around the duke. Only the duke would scratch the itch she'd started to have whenever around him.

"I would never marry a fool." Dudley had acted foolish, yes, but he had never been a fool. Some may state that there was little difference, but there was. Mr. Reeves, it seemed, was starting to appear a fool more and more. The silly man still rode ahead, unaware that they had stopped. "I know what I want." The words were out of her mouth before she could rip them back.

The duke's hungry gaze dipped to her lips. "I fear I'm more confused than ever as to what I would like."

Did he mean for a wife? For she was certainly talking about a husband. "I think if we're talking about husbands and wives, Your Grace, one ought to marry the person one desires the company most of." Just as she desired his company, his touch, his kisses, at her age, it was any wonder she was starting to feel desperate for touch, for company.

For a husband.

Days and nights filled with the act of lovemaking. Her body the last year yearned for more. Ached with a need she did not understand, but now she was starting to. For when she was around the duke, the same need and ache settled at her core, deep in her belly, and would not dissipate.

"I think you may be right," he replied, just as Mr. Reeves trotted back to them, his cheeks a rosy hue.

"Oh, do forgive me for my lack of concentration, Miss Cooper. It shall not happen again."

She pinned a half-hearted smile to her lips, and they continued on when the dowager finished speaking to Lady Leslie.

"I will dine with you tonight, Miss Cooper," the duke said, not pushing his horse forward this time to give her privacy with Mr. Reeves but staying with them. "We can play cards later, if you wish, or have some music if you like."

Expectation thrummed through her at the thought of having a night, even with the dowager present, with the duke. "That would be most welcome," she said. "I know that I am not expected anywhere this evening."

Other than with you.

. . .

*J*osh steeled himself later that evening as he sat at the head of the table, Iris and his mother at both his sides. His mother prattled on about a rumor regarding the dowager Morrison. Her ladyship had lost her husband the year before, and her misdemeanors since were starting to be significant.

Even so, he heard very little of his parent's words. His mind otherwise engaged with the lady who sat to his left.

This evening Iris wore a dress so sheer that he'd thought at first the material had been transparent. He knew he had gaped at her like a stunned deer, but he could not stop himself from admiring every morsel of her. It was time he put a name to what he was feeling for Miss Iris Cooper. *Affection. Desire. Need.*

He cared for her more than he had ever thought to care for anyone. This Season, he was determined to find a duchess, yet his attention kept moving back to Iris.

A daughter to a vicar, low on the social sphere. A woman who would not elevate his family with great connections or wealth. He had always assumed his wife would be a duke's or marquess's daughter, but a man of the cloth, that he had not imagined.

Her dress of gold tulle shimmered in the candlelight, her skin alabaster and flawless. Her eyes sparkled with delight and amusement as the conversation carried on between her and his mother.

Damn it all to hell. He was in trouble.

"I have been invited out this evening by Lady Leslie. The woman whom I addressed in the park earlier today. I'm afraid I will have to leave you to your own amusements this evening, Iris," his mother stated, glancing at him.

The pit of Josh's stomach curled and twisted with need. Iris would be alone. In his house without company. Without a chaperone. He pushed the knowledge aside. So what if she were? It did not mean that he could stay.

"Can you not put it off?" he asked his mother. Not liking the idea of being sent away and unable to spend any more time with Miss Cooper this evening. He'd wanted to play cards, or the pianoforte, or merely talk. They did that so well.

What else would they do well together?

Everything.

He picked up his wine, gulping it down. The image of her bright-blue eyes looking up at him, her lips begging for a kiss, filled his mind. He shifted on the seat, stilling his body's wayward reactions. What on earth had come over him? He was her protector, her advisor this Season. Not her seducer.

His attention slipped to her fingers as they played with the stem of her champagne glass. Long, pretty fingers, her nail scoring the glass with slow strokes.

He waved a footman over for more wine. He pulled at his cravat. Why was it ever so hot in here all of a sudden?

"I cannot. I'm sorry. I know we were going to enjoy an evening together. My maid will chaperone you, Iris."

"Of course," Miss Cooper said, her voice unable to hide the layer of disappointment in her words. "We have all Season, do we not, to play cards, or have music. I hope you enjoy your time with your friend."

"I have work to do in the office, Mother. Do you mind if I stay to finish it?"

His mother studied him a moment before she shook her head. "I do not think you should. Not until I am in residence. Tomorrow will do soon enough."

Josh cleared his throat, knowing there was no point in arguing with his parent. His hopes of staying were not appropriate. Should the *ton* find out he'd been here, at night, without his mother's presence, Miss Cooper would be married to him before he could say a word against it.

Would it be so bad if she was?

"I will collect the paperwork and leave directly," he said.

His mother stood, and he did also, bowing as she bid her goodnights to them both.

Miss Cooper threw him a cautious smile. "I shall leave you to your work, Your Grace. Thank you for today and dinner. It was very pleasant."

Josh panicked as she started to stand. He did not want their night to end. Did not want her to leave. He picked up her hand, bringing it to his lips. He kissed her gloved fingers, not missing the tremor that ran through her at his touch.

"The pleasure was all mine, Miss Cooper."

"Iris, please."

"Iris," he said aloud. The name on his lips making him all the more addled. "Goodnight," he uttered, striding from the room and starting toward the library where his office was located.

He would collect his missives and Dunsleigh's books and head back to his lodgings. He was safe there away from Miss Cooper and the temptation she wrought inside him.

Iris.

Or more to the point. Miss Cooper was safe from *him*.

CHAPTER 13

*I*ris wandered up to her room and prepared herself for bed. With the duchess out for the evening and the duke on his way back to his lodgings at Albany, there was little point to staying up.

The duchess's maid helped her into her nightdress, but not the least tired, she sat before the fire for a time, writing a letter to her mama. The house became eerily quiet and she shivered, pulling the shawl about her shoulders.

She did not particularly like being here alone. Her home in Cornwall was substantially smaller than the ducal London townhouse and was less foreboding at night, even on the rare occasions she was alone.

Iris placed her letter down, deciding to sit in the duchess's upstairs parlor, which always had a fire burning for the dowager whenever she went out for the evening, along with multiple candelabras. The room had several bookshelves, which would keep her occupied until the dowager returned home.

It did not take her long to reach the parlor, but she did not find it empty. The duke stood at the dowager's small ladies' writing desk, frowning over a letter he held in his hand.

She must have made a sound, for he glanced up quickly. "Miss Cooper. I hope I did not wake you," he said, slipping the missive into a pocket inside his evening jacket.

"Not at all." She came into the room, going to the fire and warming herself. "I was going to wait for your mama until she returned."

He strolled over to her, coming to stand before her. He was so very tall and imposing. She could not help but admire his every feature that looked carved from a master of arts. To look upon His Grace made her ache in places no lady ought.

"Do you realize you're in your nightclothes, Iris?"

The sound of her name on his lips, a deep whisper that slid over her like a caress, made her burn. And then her mind caught up to what His Grace had said, and she yelped, clutching the shawl tightly across her body.

"I must go." She turned to leave, but he clasped her arm, his fingers wrapping about her elbow, sending another shiver to pass over her. He pulled her back, closer than they were before. His eyes burned down at her, fire and determination raging in his blue orbs.

Her body shivered, heat pooled at her core. She felt her lips part. Would he kiss her?

How she wished he would. Just once. That was all she would ask for, and then he could go off and marry whomever he wanted.

"You are too beautiful for words." He reached up, running a finger across her jaw, tipping her head back. He shook his head as if he were warring within himself over something she did not know.

The one thing Iris did know was that she wanted him to kiss her. She had wanted him to kiss her if she were honest from the first time she had met the duke. So far above her. Out of her reach.

She was a vicar's daughter.

You are an earl's granddaughter.

Iris pulled together all her strength, her determination to have something she wanted above all else before entering any union that did not have the duke part of it. "You could always show me how beautiful you think me, Your Grace."

There, she had offered herself. But would he take on her proposal?

*L*ike forbidden fruit, she lured him to taste her sweetness. He should not. She was living here, under his family's roof, ensuring a good match. A suitable husband who would love her, marry her, and give her all that she deserved—happiness at last.

He had stolen that from her years before. He could not steal her innocence, her reputation from her now.

Her lips parted on an inhale of breath, and he could not deny himself one taste. Josh leaned forward, savored the slow dance toward her mouth, wanting to revel in the thought of her a little while longer.

One kiss would not ruin their friendship—her future.

Their lips touched, the lightest brush, but it wasn't enough. He covered her lips, deepening the embrace, taking her mouth as he had dreamed these past weeks.

She tasted of tea and strawberries and everything sinful.

Iris made a little gasp of pleasure but did not pull away. He ran his tongue across her bottom lip, needing to have all of her. She understood his command and opened for him like a flower in bloom.

He wrenched her against him, and he was lost. So soft,

decadent curves that called to a part of him, wild and untamed. He hardened, his breath hitched, his head spun.

What was she doing to him?

Her fingers scraped along the nape of his neck, into his hair, holding him against her. She kissed him back, her tongue mimicking his, her breaths soft, sweet pants that echoed through his soul.

Her shawl fell to the ground unheeded. He could not get enough of her. He wanted to feel her, all of her. His hands slipped over her ass, tight and firm. She moaned into his mouth, her core now hard up against his straining manhood. Josh groaned when she stirred against him, seeking a release he doubted she was even aware she could gain.

"Josh Worthingham, what do you think you're doing?" his mother's curt voice demanded from the doorway. "Unhand Miss Cooper this instant and explain yourself."

He wrenched Iris out of his hold, and without thought, he watched, horrified, as Iris tripped and fell backward onto the Aubusson rug, her bottom landing hard on the floor.

Fuckkkkk.

He reached for her, helping her stand. His heart raced to a crescendo, horrified that she may be injured.

"Tell me you are not hurt," he begged her, keeping her near him.

She shook her head, her eyes still cloudy with desire. Good sweet heaven, she was beautiful, and he wanted her still.

Josh knew what he must do. He raised his chin, facing down his parent, who looked at him with murder in her orbs. His mother closed the door, arms crossed, a fierce frown between her brows.

"Well, Your Grace? I am waiting."

Josh ground his teeth, forcing words through his lips that he'd never thought to utter. Not for Miss Cooper in any case.

"Are you not going to congratulate me, Mother? I have asked Iris to be my wife, and she has accepted me. We are to be married."

He smiled, and both women looked at him as if he were mad. Iris looked on the verge of tears, and he reached out, taking her hand, holding it firmly in his. He would never let her go. "Do not cry, my dear. Not even happy tears," he said, knowing they were not happy, but humiliated tears that ran down her cheeks.

"I have asked Miss Cooper to be my duchess, and she has agreed. Congratulate us," he stated, squeezing Iris's hand to quell her fears when she stilled beside him.

"Married. You are engaged?" the dowager duchess asked again, looking at him and Miss Cooper several times. "You were not even courting."

Josh pulled Iris closer to him, trying to stem her panic. He could feel she was on the verge of fight or flight. "I care for Iris, as she does me," he heard himself say. "The banns will be called over the next four weeks, and we shall be wed. Congratulate us, Mother, or I shall think you do not approve."

The duchess remained silent before she seemed to shake herself free of her shock. She came over to them both, hugging them in turn, and Josh knew he had fooled her. He met the shocked visage of Iris as she was pulled into a tight, congratulatory embrace from his mother.

As for Miss Cooper, she may take a little more convincing that he was not fooling her. Oh no, not at all. She would be the next Duchess of Penworth, and what a transcendent duchess she would make.

CHAPTER 14

The following day Iris sat in the Duke's library and listened to all the reasons as to why they would marry. Words such as honor demanded they marry. It was what was expected of him after being caught in such a compromising position.

A letter to her mama had been sent via express courier and the next few weeks deemed to be one of the busiest of her life. A marriage to a duke was not what she had expected when arriving in London. Nor had she expected him to kiss her last evening.

All the reasons he rattled out to her made her blood run cold. A tremor of panic rose within her that should she marry him, their marriage would be one of duty, forced wills, and not love. Not a marriage with affection, even though last night Iris had had a glimpse of what could lay between them if the duke opened his heart to her.

Where there was passion, there could be affection. She was sure of it. But the way he spoke now, no-nonsense, no emotion within his tone, merely a flat, point-by-point outlining of everything that would occur in the next few weeks. How large their wedding would be. How many guests. Who they would invite and what would happen after the wedding breakfast.

"We shall remain here for the remainder of the Season and return to Dunsleigh at its conclusion. I do not see any reason as to why we should depart. Mother and the house-keeper at Dunsleigh will guide you as to what will be required of you when managing your own home."

"While I have been raised to run a house of my own, Your Grace, Dunsleigh will be larger, I grant you, but it is still a home. I'm certain I can handle the expectations of me."

He met her gaze, raising his chin. "Have I offended you, Miss Cooper? You seem a little put out with me," he stated, watching her closely.

She fought not to roll her eyes at his aloofness, his use of her given name. Where had Iris disappeared to? Were they to be distant now? "We're to be married. Iris will do very well."

"You are angry over your name?" he pushed, wanting to know.

Not that Iris was willing to tell him. Not unless their first conversation regarding their future ended with an argument. "No one but your mama caught us kissing, Your Grace. Is it really necessary that we marry? I'm certain if you asked your mother, and I spoke with her too, she would spare us this ordeal."

He coughed, placing down his quill. "Ordeal? Is that what you think our marriage will be, Iris?" he said, using her name and blast him to hades. Her heart curled around his words, warmth spreading through her core at his use of it.

She gestured to him. "You are very businesslike. Cold and calculating. I do not like the tone of our conversation. I do not want a husband who does not feel anything for me. I came to London to look for love. That you kissed me is not my fault, and I do not see why I have to be punished by it by marrying you." There, she had said her grievances after all, and she felt better for it. He ought to know the truth now before it was too late.

It is already too late. Your mama has been written to. The duchess is demanding a wedding.

"My feelings are engaged, Iris. Our kiss stated such a fact, I thought."

His attention dipped to her lips, and she fought the urge to dampen them. Their kiss had been sweet one moment and then a kaleidoscope of need the next. To think about it now made her body throb.

"You kiss many women. I'm no fool to think you do not."

He held up his hand, halting her words. "I do not kiss many women, certainly not unmarried maids having a Season." He stood, came around the desk, and stood before her, arms crossed. He leaned against the desk, debating her.

Iris met his gaze, waited for what he would say next. "I kissed you because I like you. I kissed you because I wanted to kiss you."

Iris did not know what to do, how to react, or anything. In fact, all she could manage was to gape at him before her senses came back to rights. "You wanted to kiss me?" Did he wish to kiss her again? She wanted him to, desperately so. She may state all she liked that marriage to the duke was a bad idea, love was not what they felt for each other, but his kisses were very nice. She would not mind so much had they simply kept those up.

"I did, and I think over the next few weeks and years to come, we shall partake in a lot of it." His voice dipped to a raspy tenor that prickled her skin. "Among other things."

Iris adjusted her skirts, not wanting him to see the heat blooming on her cheeks. No man, not even Dudley, had teased her so during their engagement. She had not even kissed him before he passed away.

"All I'm trying to explain is that a marriage between us will be viewed by the *ton* as odd. They will think you have compromised me in more ways than a kiss." She stood, needing to be on eye level with the duke. "I do not want anyone to think that I came here to your home and somehow compromised you into marrying a woman far beneath your rank. Even the thought of having to face Lady Sophie Hammilyn when she hears that you are betrothed will be torturous enough."

He frowned, shaking his head at her words. "Why would it be disagreeable for Lady Sophie? I have not promised anything to the lady."

"Because if you bothered to look at her at all, you would see that she is in love with you. Pines for you and has done so since your visit to her estate last year."

"I do not want to marry Lady Sophie. I would not have offered to you if I did so. I would not have kissed you."

Iris paced over to the window and back. "You do not wish to marry me either," she retorted. "All I am saying is that I would like you to think about things for just a moment. I will marry you should I have to, but if your mama does not say a word, and we do not kiss again, I see no reason why I cannot continue my Season, find a gentleman who does want to marry me, and then I'll be out of your way forever. You shall marry a woman who fills all your requirements, and both of us will be happy."

"Is that what you truly wish for, my dear?" the dowager duchess asked, entering the room and closing the door softly behind her.

Josh groaned, pinning his mother with a disapproving glare. "Sneaking up yet again on people, are we, Mama? Your stealing about the house like some ghoul is not appreciated."

His mother came over to Iris, taking her hand. "I will not force you if you truly do not wish to marry my son, dear.

When I saw you both kissing, I assumed it was as my son stated," she said, accentuating the word. "Is it not so? Do you not wish to marry the duke?"

Iris met the duke's steely gaze, unsure what to say. In her dream world, she would marry the duke. Love him and care for him, have his children and all those wonderful things. But this was not her dream world. Their marriage would be cold with pockets of wild kisses and maybe nights too. But it would not be enough for her. She wanted her husband's heart, not a marriage born out of his honor and duty.

"While I did kiss the duke, it was a spontaneous action that was brought on by too much wine at dinner. I like the duke as a friend, but the one kiss does not warrant marriage, surely," she beseeched them both, unsure if she was getting through.

The duchess stared at them both, clearly torn. "Josh darling. Be honest with me. Had I not found you last evening, would you have proposed to Miss Cooper?"

*J*osh inwardly groaned, not wanting to answer that question at all. While he had not wanted to marry Iris, now that they were engaged, he'd warmed to the idea quite well.

Certainly, no one else had made his blood pump fast in his veins, his body to ache as it had all night, tempting him to take himself in hand. He'd not felt like that in an age, and Iris had been the one to stir his ardor.

"I would not have kissed her if I was not willing to accept any consequences of my actions."

Iris's shoulders slumped, and disappointment shone in her bright-blue eyes. She had such pretty almond-shaped orbs, her dark hair up in a loose bunch of curls atop her head just begged to be let down, admired as it lay over her undressed form.

He wanted to pull every pin from her locks, scatter them to the floor and run his hand through her hair. See it spread out over the pillows on his bed where he would make love to her until both their needs and wants were satisfied.

His determination to marry her doubled.

His mother turned to Iris, taking her hands. "You see, my dear. The duke would like to marry you if you will have him. What say you?" his parent pressed, squeezing Iris's hands. "Will you become part of our family? I know I shall love to have you as a daughter-in-law."

Iris met his eyes, and he could not tell what she was thinking, what she would say. Eventually, she sighed, just giving the smallest nod. "Very well, I shall marry the duke."

She did not sound pleased, but he would change her mind about that. The next four weeks would be filled with balls and parties, all of which he could be near her, touch her, steal kisses from her whenever he wished.

His lips twitched. The Season had just become a lot more interesting. In fact, he could not wait the several hours until tonight's Devonshire ball, where he could start introducing his future bride to the delights of the flesh.

CHAPTER 15

The duchess stood watching her son swoop his betrothed about the Devonshire ballroom. Iris appeared happy. Her bright eyes and adoring smile gave Sarah hope that their marriage would be as happy as her other children's. Josh deserved to find love, for he had so much to give. He merely needed to find the right woman to bestow it upon.

Her only child to remain unwed, and the family heir needed to marry, secure the line with a child and continue the proud Worthingham, Penworth name for another generation.

"Good evening, Your Grace," Lady Sophie said, dipping into a curtsy before standing beside her.

Sarah inclined her head in welcome. "Good evening, Lady Sophie. I did not know you were in attendance. Is your father here with you? I have not seen him about of late."

"Oh, he's over there," she said, gesturing to the farther side of the room. "I came to congratulate you on the duke's engagement to Miss Cooper. How happy you must be."

"I am very happy, yes," she said, relieved that her feelings on the forthcoming nuptials were genuine. In fact, she could hardly contain her excitement that her favorite friend would soon be related to her by marriage. Their children married. One could not hope for more.

"I should like to make a match this year. If Miss Cooper can find love, I'm certain I can too, do you not think?"

"Of course," the duchess replied, uncertain as to what Lady Sophie could mean by such words and not particularly wishing to know. Did she believe Iris to be beneath her? Surprised that she had found her match so quickly?

"Being the age we both are, and Miss Cooper older than myself by several years, I should think she is of similar age to the duke. I do pray that she will be a good, abiding wife, give you many grandchildren."

The duchess narrowed her eyes, pinning Lady Sophie with a hardened stare. "I do not see why she should not. Seven and twenty is not old, Lady Sophie."

Lady Sophie's amused laugh rang false, and Sarah understood what this little tête-à-tête was about. The duchess had to stop herself from grinding her teeth.

"I merely mention such a thing because if you remember, Lady Astley several years back married when she was seven and twenty and was unable to give the earl any children. Very sad," Lady Sophie said with a pout and considering glance at the duke and Miss Cooper, who twirled past them.

"I do not think that will be the case with my son or future daughter-in-law, Lady Sophie," she stated, her tone hard but not cruel. "I shall let the duke and Miss Cooper know that you wish them well and happiness."

Lady Sophie raised her glass of champagne, toasting the air. "Of course, I would appreciate that, Your Grace," she said.

The duchess left her then, unsure she liked what Lady Sophie said or the reasons behind it. Not that she believed in any of the words spoken, but she was not fooled enough not to know that Lady Sophie had wanted to marry her son and was probably a little slighted that she had not landed him.

But would she spread such rumors about Iris? Ensure the *ton* gossiped about Iris's age? Although a little older than most debutantes, Iris was certainly not over the hill and ready to be put to pasture.

One thing she was thankful for was that it was not Lady Sophie who had been caught kissing the duke. Marriage to such a woman would have left her son regretting his choice, but the duchess could not see that happening with Iris.

No, they were already friends and soon would be lovers. That solid base was enough to weld a solid foundation for a happy future.

An unbreakable bond of love.

*I*ris had lost count of how many people she had greeted and thanked during the ball. Her betrothal to the duke had increased her popularity tenfold. Women who had not spoken to her all Season were now flocking to her side.

She supposed she was no longer competition and was now suitable enough to be associated with. That she would soon be a duchess did not hurt her chances of friendship either.

All but one woman came up to them. Lady Sophie. The one lady who had reached out the hand of friendship to her not a week past was now distant.

Why she would react in such a cold way to the news of her betrothal, she could only come to one conclusion. That lady had wanted the duke for herself. Was put out that a woman such as Iris had been the one he proposed to.

If only Lady Sophie knew the truth of it all. Not that their union was a love match, far from it. He'd merely made the mistake of kissing her and had been caught. Had he not been so forward, they would never have married.

The knowledge left her cold, and she thrust the depressing realization aside, set on enjoying her waltz with her husband-to-be. In just one month she would be the Duchess of Penworth. No one would look upon her with pity after the fact.

At least she had the duke to thank for that. Her scar on her temple ignored, and her injured leg and resulting limp no longer signifying a remark or sympathizing glance. Not as a duchess. The name would protect her from snide remarks or such looks, one thing she hated most when in society.

"You appear quite lost in thought, Iris. Care to share what you are thinking of?" the duke asked, an amused light in his eyes.

Iris saw no reason not to be truthful. "I was thinking about how your name will protect me from those who would wish to remind me of my faults. My scars, both physical and visual, for one thing. I will no longer have to endure any comments or sad, pouty faces when they happen to notice it."

The duke visibly paled, and Iris pulled him promptly to the side of the room. "Your Grace? Are you unwell?" she asked him, hoping he was not coming down with some malady or some such ailment.

He gestured for a footman and snatched a glass of champagne, downing it. What on earth had come over him that he appeared so out of sorts?

"It is nothing. Come," he said, pulling her through the throng of guests and out of the ballroom. He led her down a deserted passage somewhere in the bowels of Devonshire House.

They passed room after darkened room, the muffled sound of the ball a distant hum. The noise of a door shutting farther along the hall made her gasp, and the duke pulled her into a closet, shutting the door not long before the tap of shoes sounded nearby.

She could make out his features by a small window high in the room, and she could see that he was smiling, waiting for whoever was outside to leave.

"Even betrothed, I should not be alone in here with you." His whispered words made her stomach flutter, her heart thumped hard in her chest. He smelled delicious, as fresh as lemon verbena. She wanted his touch on her skin, wanted him to close the small space between them and show her again what it was like to be in his arms.

Kissed with abandonment but without interruption.

The last few days, she had thought of what would have happened had the dowager not found them.

She shivered and then gasped as he clasped her hip, walking her back until she came up hard against the wall.

"Our last kiss was interrupted," he said, tipping her chin up with his finger. "This one will not be."

Her breath came in short pants. Iris ran her fingers atop his superfine coat, clasping the lapels of his jacket and pulling him toward her. There was no point in playing coy. She wasn't the type of woman to pretend she did not want what he offered. She had dreamed of being his wife, and soon she would be. There was no harm in taking what he offered and enjoying every decadent, delicious moment of his touch.

His mouth. On hers. His warmth enveloping and consuming her all at once.

He dipped his head, and she ached for the kiss to commence.

Oh yes, being his duchess would be no challenge, no heartache at all.

CHAPTER 16

*I*ris felt willing and warm under his touch, and he wanted to touch her. Everywhere he could and before he made her his legally before God. His body burned to eliminate her words that had spiked so much guilt within him only minutes ago on the ballroom floor. His only thought had been removing them from the room and having her in his arms where no past regrets rose to haunt him.

It had been too long since he'd held her. Their last kiss, as short and sweet as it had been, had left him wanting more, and he'd not been able to distract himself. Not with riding, walking, visiting his club—nothing cured his need to be around her.

His response and mood had been odd and vexing.

But now, with Iris back in his grip, he understood why he'd been feeling so off. He lusted after his future bride. The next weeks would be arduous indeed, but then, once they were married, he could enjoy her, bring her to such heights that she would lust after him every minute of every day too.

Her tongue swept against his, her kiss as frantic and

commanding as his own. His hands were everywhere, the silk of her gown no impediment to his need.

He wanted to feel all of her, tease and love her as she deserved.

"We should not be in here. What if someone catches us again?"

Josh reached back, snipping the lock on the door. "That will keep anyone at bay."

She threw him a dubious look. "What makes you think they will not simply wait outside until we leave, and then we shall have to answer for our actions."

He shrugged, reaching for her again. She did not shy away from his touch. If anything, she melted into it. Her breasts pushed against his silk waistcoat, the tight pebbles of her nipples teasing him to lathe them with his mouth.

Not yet. Not here, his mind warned.

Josh dipped his head, kissing the whorl of her ear, the sensitive skin beneath her lobe. Her hands tightened about his hips, and he breathed deep her delicious scent. Now his favorite.

What was happening to him?

"You smell so good," he spoke, unable to think of anything more delicate and pretty to say what he meant. He doubted he could speak with a poetic verse, for she had his mind blown. "When we're married, I'm going to taste every part of you, Iris," he promised her, moving to the fleshy mounds of her breasts at her bodice.

When he'd seen her this evening, his heart had stopped at the sight of her. So beautiful, he had physically ached at the vision she made. He'd wanted to strip her of her gown and have her for himself, not escort her to another ball where others would enjoy what was his.

He'd found his bride. He wanted to have her all to himself.

Her fingers spiked through his hair. She lay her head against the wall, giving him leave to do as he pleased, without a word spoken.

He could not let her leave him without having one taste of her. Josh slipped her gown down over one breast, exposing her.

Her breasts were ample, a lovely handful and then some. He ran the pad of his finger about her nipple, transfixed as it pebbled harder still. Her chest rose and fell with labored breaths, and he glanced up to see her biting her lip, watching his every move.

"Do you like what you see, Your Grace?" she boldly asked him.

His cock hardened at her sultry words, and he took a calming breath, fighting the urge to take more of her tonight. "Fuck yes, I like what I see, and it is mine to do with as I please."

She made a half moan, half gasp before his mouth was on her again, suckling her sweet nipple into his mouth. He teased her with his tongue, relished every squirm, and thrust into his mouth.

His mind thought of all the things he wanted to do to her. How he had to wait what seemed like forever before he could have her alone, all night, without the fear of interruption.

He wanted her with a need that both scared and fascinated him. She wasn't what he thought he wanted. Unsuitable in so many ways, but with her in his arms, her touch that drove his senses wild, her gasps and breathy sighs against his ear drove him mad. She may not have been what he thought he wanted, but he certainly wanted her now. Iris would be his wife and soon.

Just not soon enough.

. . .

*J*n the early hours of the morning, the duke escorted Iris and his mother back to the London townhouse. The servants already going about their workday, lighting fires, and preparing breakfast.

"I am for bed, my dears. I shall see you later this afternoon," the duchess said, not bothering to ask what they were about.

Iris turned to the duke. Sure he, too, would leave and gain some sleep. Her feet ached, but surprisingly, her leg did not, a nice change to her normal routine. Maybe with all the extra exercise she'd been partaking in of late, the dancing, walking, and riding, her leg agreed with the action. Maybe being idle in Cornwall was not what was best for her.

"Come, breakfast with me," he whispered against her neck, sending a shiver of delight down her spine. She met his gaze, wanting to lean back into his body behind her.

"I would like that," she replied, reaching back and taking his hand, pulling him toward the dining room. He kissed the top of her gloved fingers, and her heart did a little flip in her chest. How was it that the man walking beside her was hers? She could not quite believe the truth of it all.

The table was set with the finest silverware, flowers, and a large fruit platter adorned the center. Four footmen stood at the corners of the room, ready to serve.

Iris sat beside the duke, who seated himself at the head of the table, catching the eye of one of the servants. "You may serve," he commanded the staff.

Iris's stomach rumbled at the sight and smell of bacon, ham, eggs, and freshly cooked bread.

The duke chuckled, reaching around and tipping her face toward him. "Had I known you were that hungry, Iris, I would have brought you home sooner."

Iris bit her lip, not so much hungry for the food on her

plate but the man at her side. How delicious it was to be the center of his notice. "I enjoyed the ball. Parts of it were very pleasant indeed. I would not want to have left," she admitted, liking the wicked grin he bestowed on her.

"I did not want to leave either," he admitted, letting her go and putting a respectable distance between them again. "Not the closet, at least."

She chuckled as the servants finished attending them, pouring Iris a cup of tea and the duke a coffee.

"You may leave." The duke dismissed them, and they left without a word, closing the door behind them.

The duke picked up his coffee, sipping it. Iris could feel his eyes on her, watching her. She wondered what he saw. Was he pleased with whom he was marrying? Did he really mean what he said about enjoying her kisses?

After what they had done in the closet at the ball, she could not imagine that he did not. No man kissed a woman with such passion and did not care for her. Even if that care was innocuous right now, it could grow, bloom into so much more if she were blessed a second time in her life.

"We will be married in only a few weeks. I want to use that time to get to know you more. I believe we are not expected at any entertainment this evening, so I was hoping tomorrow morning you would be up for a ride in Hyde Park without Mother. I will bring a groom as chaperone, of course."

Iris swallowed the slice of bacon she was nibbling on. A morning at the park with the duke, when there would be few ladies present and a groom, no dowager duchess. "What would you like to know about me, Your Grace? I could answer any questions that you like if you wanted to start now."

He leaned back in his chair, rubbing his jaw in thought. "What is your favorite pastime?"

"Well, I once would have said reading, but after last evening, I would have to say kissing you."

Shock registered on the duke's handsome face. His eyes burned with a need that she had also to her very soul. Her body did not feel like itself. It was all fidgety and eager.

She wanted more kisses, more of his touch.

The memory of his tongue laving her nipple almost made her groan. He clasped her hand, pulling her from her chair and wrenching her onto his lap. Iris gasped, feeling the hardness of his member jutting through the evening breeches he still wore. She pressed against it, a delicious warmth settling between her legs.

"There are going to be more kisses, Iris," he growled, his mouth taking hers in a punishing embrace. Iris threw herself into kissing him, having wanted to do nothing but kiss the man since his mouth left hers several hours ago.

What was this madness that thrummed through her veins and would not be sated?

To know that she would have her whole life in his arms thrilled her. How had her fortune changed so much in the last few weeks? She had not dreamed of coming to London and becoming betrothed to a duke.

A kind and passionate one as hers was turning out to be.

The start to their courtship may not have been conventional, but she was determined to make him happy. Make them both so, and give him lots of children.

She broke the kiss, wrapping her arms around his neck. "I do hope so," she replied, kissing the duke this time, reveling in his taste, his heat, and ardent response. Because now that she had a taste of His Grace, she would be loath to lose it.

CHAPTER 17

*J*osh had not meant to haul Iris onto his lap. To kiss her again so soon or demand his servants leave them, which no doubt right about now was fodder for gossip below stairs. He could just imagine the size of the hornet's nest he had disturbed.

But seeing her seated beside him, nibbling on her bacon had been too much to bear, and he'd snatched her onto his lap, determined to have her close, just for a little while longer until they parted company for the day.

He wished he could stay here, sleep under the same roof, but it would not be safe to do so. Such an action would tarnish her reputation. But until he left, he would make use of the close proximity and have her all to himself and in any way he wished.

Still, the idea of sneaking into the house late at night, stealing into her room and laying her bare, stripping her of her night rail or gown made him groan. He wanted nothing more than to slide her free of her silk stockings. Work his fingers through the ribbons of her corset, setting her ample bosom free for his kiss.

He lifted her, pushing the plates to the side of the table and seating her atop the mahogany. She gasped but did not try to stop him. She should, of course. He wanted to have her here in the dining room without thought of who could come in or what would be said.

Fire coursed through his blood. His cock felt heavy and hard in his breeches. "Touch me," he begged. If he could not have her fully, he needed her in this way.

Her eyes gleamed with fiery promise, and then the slow, tentative touch of her fingers grazed the outside of his breeches. He fought not to demand her to take him in hand harder, stroke him until he came. Instead, he leaned his forehead against hers, watching as she learned every part of his cock.

"You're so hard, Your Grace." She bit her lip, and he clenched his jaw.

The sight of her teeth clasping the small piece of flesh drove him mad. He imagined lifting her silk gown to pool at her waist, stroke the wetness between her legs until she squirmed for more. Begged to be fucked.

She flipped the buttons to his falls open and reached into his breeches. A guttural moan wrenched from him, a sound he had never heard before, not in all the times he'd been with other women. He pumped into her touch, her fingers long and banded tight about him, helping him find pleasure.

"What will happen to you when I do this?" she asked him, still fascinated by his cock that strained and grew in her hold.

"I'll spend against your dress, and we cannot be having that," he said, covering her hand with his and stopping her.

She pouted, and he took her lips, wanting her so much that he thought he might die. How was he ever to survive the time before their wedding?

Her thumb rubbed over the tip of his cock, and she lifted

her fingers, staring at the transparent liquid. "Fascinating," she stated, her tongue darting out to taste him.

Good God, he would expire. Who was this woman? The siren in his arms did not appear to be the shy, sugary-sweet woman he'd met at the beginning of the Season. This woman did not shy away from pleasure but wanted to experience and learn all that he could show her.

He could not wait to be hers in truth.

"I like the taste of you, Your Grace."

"You would taste better," he returned, tying his falls back up and placing well-needed distance between them. His chest rose and fell with labored breaths.

"I will not deflower my future bride on the dining table. We must behave," he demanded, needing to rein in his desires, for he would allow her to do anything to him, so long as he was able to play with her in return.

"Pity," she quipped, slipping off the table and starting for the door. "It would have been as memorable as the closet last evening. Good day, Your Grace," she said, grinning over her shoulder and leaving him standing, gaping after her as she left him alone.

There were too many weeks left before she became his wife.

"*D*o you have it, Father?" Lady Sophie commanded, her voice harsh and impatient as she snatched the rolled parchment from her father's hand. She opened it, scanning the black scrawl that ran over the page.

She laughed, the sound calculating. "La, how the dear Miss Cooper will find what I hold in my hands disappointing. I should think being the daughter of a vicar, she would not appreciate her betrothed had a hand in Redgrove's death."

"The baron's death was his own fault. The young man was always partaking in bets. It was only a matter of time before he came to an unfortunate end," her father stated, starting for the library.

Sophie followed close on his heels. "That does not signify. The duke will not be marrying Miss Cooper from silly old Cornwall."

"She is the Earl Buttersworth's granddaughter. Do not forget that, Sophie, even if the family is estranged."

She shrugged, slumping down on the leather settee before the roaring fire. "The countess wants nothing to do with her granddaughter after Lady Jane married a boring old vicar. How droll."

"Lady Jane fell in love. I worry that this course you are taking is not right, Sophie. You are an earl's daughter yourself. There are other dukes, marquesses, and earls in society you could marry tomorrow. What is it about Penworth that you're so fascinated with?"

She bit her lip, not wanting to tell her father it was a simple purpose. The duke did not want her. The diamond of the Season. One of the most beautiful and adequately dowered daughters in England. No, he wanted the scarred, lame Miss Iris Cooper from nowhere. A woman who she had seen herself limp when no one else had noticed. "He will not be happy with Miss Cooper. Not in a year or so. He will regret his hasty choice. I am equal to him in wealth and position. We suit much better and I have always loved the ducal coronet I've seen the dowager duchess wear at times. It will suit my coloring more than Miss Boring Cooper."

Her father sighed, pinning her with one of his disapproving stares. She ignored his warning.

"It is already done, Sophie. They are engaged. You cannot come between them now, no matter the fact that I have given you that note out of fatherly affection."

She read down the torn bet from the book at Whites. So many years ago, but the words were as clear now as they were then. The bet that the duke had placed, one hundred pounds to anyone who could beat his time about Hyde Park in a curricle.

What a pity that it was the duke's newly betrothed's lost love who had taken up the call. Had raced about the park with carelessness and killed himself in the process and almost killing Miss Cooper along with him.

What would the sweet, angelic Miss Cooper say when she hears the duke, her future husband, had been the mastermind to her injuries? To her betrothed's death.

"Miss Cooper will not remain engaged to the duke with this knowledge. And then he shall be free to marry a woman suitable to his rank. That woman will be me. No one in society would dare try to cut me off from having what I want."

"Do not be so manipulative, Sophie, or I shall send you back to Hampshire. You must not cause trouble in town. I will not have it. You're a lady. You must act like one."

"I will not cause trouble, and you can be certain that I shall act with the utmost care. Miss Cooper will never know that it is I who has given her this information. No one will trace it to you or me, Papa. But you do wish to have what I want, do you not? You would not deny me happiness."

Her father pointed at the parchment as if it were something alive and dangerous. "I should not have taken it, and if anyone should find out, I will lose my position at Whites. Never to be accepted there or any other gentleman's club. Be sure that it is not traced to us if you're so determined to have the duke as your husband. Although, in my opinion, I did not see the attachment you seem so certain was between you. Are you sure you're not mistaken and have confused friendship with more?"

She frowned, rolling up the bet and starting from the room. "Of course, I know the difference. The duke would not have called on us had he not wanted to further his acquaintance with me. That is not the way of a gentleman."

Her father shook his head. "Very well, do what you must, but this better not go awry for our family, Sophie, or it'll not just be the *ton* whom you will have to face, but my wrath as well."

She threw her father a sweet smile, knowing when she did, she always got her way. His features softened, and she knew he'd already forgiven her and trusted her words. "I promise it will not. All will be well, Papa, and soon you will have a duchess as a daughter. How pleasing that sounds."

She flounced from the room, starting for her own. Tomorrow night was the Morrison masquerade ball. She would start her plan then, small tidbits of questions, little doubts in Miss Cooper's ears, so when she did finally read the bet, she would know the truth of her past and her future.

Sophie smiled, excitement thrumming through her veins. Her Grace, Sophie Worthingham, Duchess of Penworth had a special, perfect sound to it. She would enjoy being a pillar, one of society's highest-ranked hostesses. Married to Penworth, she would rule all of London if for no other reason than she wanted it to be so.

CHAPTER 18

*I*ris and the dowager duchess arrived at the Morrison's masquerade ball dressed specifically as their hostess the dowager countess had specified on the invitations.

The theme was the royal court of Versailles, an opulent and extravagant mask for anyone to attend. Yet, the duchess had procured Iris a gown that was beyond her expectations, delivered and sized a day before the event. A marvel that she still could not grasp had occurred. It was told other attendees started to plan their gowns months before they traveled to London for the Season.

The gold, embroidered silk frock had roses stitched into the fabric. Although not entirely correct for the royal court of France, the empire cut was nonetheless a beautiful, opulent gown.

Her black cloak had a gold silk ribbon stitched about the hems and complemented the dress. Her mask, however, was a piece of art. The brightest blue silk she'd ever seen and covered in multicolored paste jewels, it sat across her eyes and nose, her hair hidden under a highly perched wig that ladies would have worn a century before.

Iris caught sight of herself as they entered the ballroom and could not recognize the woman she saw. Would Josh pick her out from the many people here? The noise, laughter, and dancing somewhat rowdier than other balls she had attended caught her by surprise. How anyone could continue a conversation in this uproar was a miracle maker.

"Does Lady Morrison allow everyone who wishes to attend to come to her masks? Was that not the way of some of the French masquerade balls?" she asked the duchess as they made their way over to where several chaise lounges sat against the wall.

"I believe so, so do keep your guard. Anyone this evening may be present, and not everyone a person of good standing."

The duchess sat, but Iris remained standing, her leg today protesting whenever she sat still for too long. Iris flicked open her fan, waving it slowly before her face as she watched the *ton* at play.

This would be her life now. After she married the duke, they would attend the Season, host balls and parties each year. Several acquaintances joined them, laughing when they realized who Iris and the duchess were, since their costumes made it so very hard to decipher their identity.

Iris kept a vigil on who arrived. No names were announced since the ball was based on mystery. The revelers kept Iris entertained. She did not miss admiring the beautiful jewels, the rich, colorful dominos, or the guests who snuck away into darkened corners and not returning for several minutes.

But where was her betrothed? Surely he would be here soon. She did not look so different that he would not know how to find her.

A gentleman bowed before her, and Iris recognized him

to be Lord Templedon. His mask was one held by his hand and he pulled it away from his face.

He smiled, but something about his glee seemed false to Iris. Why, she could not say, merely what she felt. "Miss Cooper. You are utterly breathtaking. Please say you will dance with me?"

She held out her hand, letting him lead her onto the floor. "I did not think you would recognize me, my lord. It seems my costume is not as good as I thought it."

"I would recognize you anywhere," he stated, his tone serious.

Iris ignored his words, letting him pull her into the Strawberries and Cream lineup. What on earth had come over him to say something like that, especially as all of London now knew she was engaged to Penworth?

"This is my first mask, and what I've seen of it so far is enthralling. Have you attended one before?" she asked Templedon, wanting to keep the conversation light and appropriate.

"Many, but until tonight, they have not had the allure as this ball does." He pulled her into a spin before the dance separated them a moment. The dance kept them apart for several steps before moving up the line together. "Masks are for inhibitions to be ignored, hidden under cover of cloaks and mystery," he whispered against her ear, his lips skimming her flesh.

Iris pulled away, putting space between them. "I fear you shall be disappointed in me, my lord. I shall enjoy the ball, but that is where my excessive nature ends."

They had stopped dancing, and several other couples tried to hurry them along as the dance required their presence. It was of little use. She could not continue to dance with a man who thought she was open to a rendezvous with him.

A hand slipped about her waist, and her trepidation over the conversation evaporated at the touch of her betrothed.

She glanced at the duke but found him staring down Templedon, anger thrumming off him in waves.

"Templedon, if you will excuse us," he said, his tone hard and brooking no argument.

Templedon, Iris noticed, did not look the least perturbed by the duke's words. Iris readily went with him, but he did not return her to his mother's side. Instead, he walked them to the terrace doors that were pushed open to allow the cooling night air to enter.

He did not say a word as they made their way out onto the flagstone terrace, guests of the ball outside here too drinking, laughing, and dancing as much as those indoors.

"I see that I will have to ensure you are never alone with rogues such as Templedon trying to woo you into his bed. I hope you were not tempted, Miss Cooper."

They stopped near the end of the terrace, still within view of the other guests but far enough away to speak privately. "Oh, I was tempted, Your Grace. How could I not be?" she teased him, wanting him to feel a fool at having even asked her such a question. She was marrying him, not Templedon. Had she wanted to marry the earl, she would have.

The duke frowned, a muscle at his temple flexing. "Are you in earnest?" he asked her, his tone both shocked and what she hoped was a small amount of fear.

Iris checked that no one was watching them and stepped closer to His Grace. Close enough that both their cloaks hid her hand. She caught hold of the waistband of his silk breeches, dragging him against her. "No, I am not, but you should know that I am not. Only one man tempts me, and it is not Templedon."

Heat blazed in Josh's eyes, his chest rose and fell, and she felt every ounce of the control he wielded starting to crack.

She knew he wanted to kiss her. She could all but taste his need, for she too felt the same.

When they were married, she promised herself, she would kiss him wherever and whenever she liked.

"Tell me who tempts you, Iris. I must hear it from your lips."

She grinned, slipping her finger behind the waist of his breeches, teasing him. "You do," she admitted but a breath from his lips. They were so close, all but a sway from brushing their lips together.

If only she could kiss him here and now. Throw caution aside, propriety and etiquette, and do what she wanted. But she could not. Not yet, at least.

Iris stepped back, leaning against the terrace railing. "Now, you must explain to me why you would ask such a question. Is it not obvious who I want? I thought after several interludes, you knew my desires."

*A*ll true, and Josh felt foolish for having reacted in the way he had. He had never wanted to injure someone as severely as he'd wanted to pummel Lord Templedon after viewing him on the ballroom floor, a scant breath from Iris's neck. Had the bastard kissed her there? He could not ask her that now, but he would not allow anyone to touch her again if he could ensure it.

He rolled his shoulders, forcing himself to relax. Her words had gone someway in soothing his ruffled feathers, but he could not overcome the feeling he had acted a jealous cur.

Who was he fooling? He had been a jealous bastard ready to draw blood at the sight of Iris so close to the rake Templedon. It had taken all his good breeding and determination not to demand retribution on a field at dawn. The sight of

Iris in his arms had been a physical blow to his gut, and he hated the memory of it.

He glanced down at the flagstones at his feet, fighting to find the words to explain himself. It was not Iris's fault that Templedon wanted her. Hell, Josh wanted her more but could not have her.

Yet.

But soon. Soon she would be his in name, promised before God to love and cherish their union forever.

"I apologize if I overreacted to seeing you with Templedon. I did not like his familiarity with you."

Her lips twitched. "Are you admitting to feeling jealous, Your Grace?" she boldly asked him, pinning him with a knowing look.

He swallowed, having never admitted such a thing to anyone ever in his life before. "There may have been a tidbit of jealousy, but," he erred, "it was more closely related to anger toward Templedon that he dared have you so close to him."

She tipped her head to the side, studying him. "I do not believe so. You were jealous, which, I will admit, pleases me. I know I would not like seeing you dance with another woman, letting her whisper inappropriate things in your ear."

Anger spiked through him again, and he came up to her, clasping her hips. "Did the rogue do such a thing?" he asked, looking back toward the ballroom. "I will call him out."

She chuckled, her hands finding his and clasping them tightly. "What does it matter what he did? I do not want Templedon." She tugged him closer. "I want you."

He schooled himself to behave. To not drag her into the gardens and show her too just how much he wanted her. Josh looked out onto the darkened grounds, full of hidden, shadowy places, rethinking his plan. It was the perfect location for a tryst.

"I want to be alone with you." Never before had he wanted to slip away from a ball, leave without notice and have his way with a woman not used to such assignations. Iris tugged at a part of him that he had not known existed before meeting her.

He wondered for a moment what he would have done had she married Redgrove and they were introduced, circulated in the same social set. Would he have had the same reaction to her presence as he did now? As if his soul was calm and crazed all at the same time by simply being near her? Would he have tried to persuade her to enjoy an amorous affair?

Something told him he would have and not cared a hoot whom he injured so long as she was his for any amount of time.

"There are too many people about, and no matter the masks we wear or cloaks, everybody knows who we are. We will be seen."

"What does it matter?" he argued. "We're to be married. A little pre-wedding scandal is not so bad."

She chuckled, again looking to see who was around them. A wicked light entered her eyes, and he knew she would do as he asked. Give him what he wanted.

Her in his arms.

"What shall I tell the duchess? If we're to have time alone, it cannot be here. I will not embarrass the duchess with scandal. No matter," she said, tapping his nose quickly, "how much you tempt me."

Josh pursed his lips. "Tell Mama you have a megrim and would like to leave. I will escort you home. Mother will not suspect. We will steal a moment or two alone then."

She nodded once. "I will go tell her now. Come, you must help me."

He followed her, not wanting to let her out of his sight. Not with all the hungry rogues who seemed to think now that she was his that she was some kind of sport—a woman to conquer and steal away from under him.

Well, they would not succeed. Miss Iris Cooper was his, and they all better learn that lesson before he had to teach them a harder one.

With his fists.

CHAPTER 19

fter telling the duchess of her headache, Iris made her way to the foyer of the London home, a feat that took far longer than she would like. Her body thrummed with expectation. Soon, she would be alone with Josh. Would he return her to his home? Or would they go someplace else?

They could not go to his bachelor lodgings, someone would definitely see them there, and then the scandal would be too great to bear.

Josh ordered the carriage to be brought around, and it wasn't long before he'd helped her up into the equipage and they were off.

He turned and opened the little portal under the driver's box, giving orders before closing it again and facing her.

The carriage was dark and made all the more so when the duke untied the curtains above the windows and sealed them off from the world.

Iris took a calming breath, her stomach fluttering at the thought of what they were about to do. He would kiss her, that she understood. But would he do more than that? Would he kiss her breast again?

She bit her lip, heat pooling between her legs at the thought of him doing so.

Josh moved over beside her, cupping her face in his hands. "I do not think I will ever have enough of you," he admitted. He moved to kiss her, the action painfully slow. Too slow for Iris.

Iris met him halfway. She needed to feel him, kiss him as she had longed to do from the moment he left her the day before.

The instant their lips touched, an explosion of emotions tore through her, and she wanted to take all she could from him. Lose herself in his touch, his intoxicating kiss that urged and teased her.

Her breathing hitched, her breasts swelled, the bodice of her gown feeling restrictive. The night she would lay with him for the first time would be a magical dream, and how she counted down the time until they could be alone.

The carriage rolled around a corner, pushing her against him. The duke lay back against the squabs, urging her upon him. Iris sat back, untying the ribbon at the front of her domino and stripping herself of her cloak. It was only then that she realized she still wore her mask. Pulling it from her face, she watched as his dark, hungry gaze devoured her.

She shivered, coming over him, taking his lips in a searing kiss. Her emotions rioted within her. How could she be so enamored with a man she had only known a few weeks?

The admission made little sense, but as true as she was kissing him, falling for the duke more and more each day, so too were her feelings. They grew each time he walked into a room. A little wedge of her heart burst to life at every kind word, sweet gesture, or wicked kiss.

If Iris were not careful, she would soon be in love with her husband. But would he love her in return?

His hands slid down her back, hauling her against his

hard manhood. Iris wanted to see him, feel and play, but a carriage was not the place, no matter how much she longed to be so with Josh.

"I want to touch you. Let me please you, Iris."

His whispered plea pulled at a part of her she had not known existed. She nodded, trusting him and needing him beyond reason. Her body burned aflame, ached to be loved, and it was time it was.

*J*osh fought with his conscience. He should not be here. Should not have his betrothed writhing in his lap in unsated lust before they were married. But nor could he deny them both what they wanted.

And he wanted her.

He wanted every part of her, body and soul. She was such a beautiful woman, inside and out, with a heart of gold and a face as sweet as an angel's. Who would not lust after such a woman? That this woman was his made him the luckiest bastard in London.

And he was a bastard. He had caused her so much pain and grief in her short life. He would make amends, and he would start by loving her as a woman ought to be loved.

He would make her life happy, easy just as she deserved and in time, pay for the sins he billed against her.

Josh rucked up her gown, needing to feel her. His hands skimmed her shift, moving it out of the way. She stilled in his hold when his fingers sliced over her mons, the hairs at the apex of her thighs tickling his hand.

She was wet, hot, and ready. He could take her now, fuck her, and he doubted she would feel any discomfort, would deny him.

"You're ready for me, my darling," he said, slipping two

fingers to run across her aching seam. She ground against him, her body seeking release.

"How do you know?" she whispered against his ear, making him shiver. He steeled himself to behave. To not rip open his front falls and sheathe himself into her willing heat.

Fuck her in the carriage like a trollop from Pall Mall. Like a man unable to control the lust, the need that coursed through his blood.

He teased her flesh, circling her core before dipping his finger into her cunny. Her eyes widened, and the pit of his gut clenched. "You like that?" he stated, knowing that she did. "You're weeping for me between your legs. That's how I know."

She nodded, pushing down a little on his hand, taking him farther.

Josh groaned, helping her ride him. He flicked his thumb over her beaded nubbin, wishing that it was his cock that sank into her depths. That took her to the peak of pleasure she was climbing to.

She moaned his name, and his cock begged for release, but not tonight. Tonight, right at this exquisite moment, it was all for Iris. He wanted to bring her to a climax. Watch as she came apart in his arms.

Iris became a woman in his arms, riding him, taking what she wanted. Josh held her, simply laid back, and enjoyed the view she made. He would never tire of seeing her like this. Tonight was just the beginning of many enjoyable carriage rides in their future they could take.

Her hands clutched his shoulders, her eyes closed, a little frown of concentration between her brows as she worked her way to release.

"Have you ever climaxed before?" he asked.

She shook her head, her eyes glazed with want.

"Sit back," he commanded, helping her to move to the space at Josh's side. "I want to make you shatter. I want to lick you until you grind against my tongue and take what you want."

Her mouth popped open, and she gaped at him. "What do you mean?" she asked, but continued to shift off his lap to do as he ordered.

"You will see. Now lay back," he commanded, his mouth salivating at the thought of tasting her.

She did as he bade without question. Josh slid her gown up her legs, taking his time in kissing her sweet, long legs as he went. The musky scent teased his senses. Her skin tasted of jasmine soap. She was everything delicious and right.

He pooled her gown at her waist, exposing her to him. She wore no pantalets, her sex exposed to him, weeping for his touch.

Fuck, she was wet.

Josh pushed her legs apart and grinned at the soft, rosy hue that kissed her cheeks. "Do not be embarrassed, my darling. I'm going to do this a lot when we're married. You will soon grow used to it."

She nodded again, biting her lip, driving him to distraction. He bent over her, pulling her to the edge of the seat, exposing her further. "So tempting, so delicious. I'm going to eat you until you scream."

"Do it then," she taunted. "Do it now."

Josh needed no further prodding. He kissed her cunny, lathing her engorged nubbin with a ferocity that he had never experienced before. Her scent was an elixir on his tongue. She tasted like sweet wine and everything unspoiled.

Her gasp of pleasure almost made him spend in his breeches. He suckled on her nubbin, teasing her opening with his tongue, fucking her with his mouth with unrelenting need.

"You taste so good," he moaned, already planning when they could be alone together like this. Three weeks before their wedding was too long away.

"You feel wonderful," she replied, taunting him more.

What a wicked woman his wife would be; he could not wait to make her so. Josh lifted her legs to rest atop his shoulders, sensing the movement did not pain her. She undulated against his face, working herself against his tongue as much as he served her weeping cunny.

She made mewling sounds, his name on her lips driving him to distraction. He knew she was close. He kissed her harder, fucking her with his hand as well as his tongue, and she screamed, her fingers scoring through his hair as she rode his face in pleasure.

Josh lathed her flesh until the last of her tremors ran their course through her body. She went limp in his hold, and he sat back, settling her skirts about her body once again.

"Did you enjoy your first taste of pleasure, my darling wife-to-be?" he asked, coming to sit beside her and helping her set to rights the bodice of her gown. He reached down to the floor, picking up her cloak and folding it in his lap.

"Can such pleasure happen every time we're together? On our wedding night, or when we... When we—"

"Make love for the first time." He smiled, taking pity on her. "I should hope that will happen to both of us every time. I would not be doing my duty if I did not please my wife." He tipped up her chin, staring into the bluest eyes he'd ever beheld. Eyes he knew one could lose oneself in if they allowed it. "And I intend to please you. In all ways."

She smiled at him, clearly pleased at his words. "I think I shall like being married to you. How long until we are wed?" she asked him.

He pulled her against him, wanting her close as the carriage meandered its way through London, taking the long way back to the Penworth townhouse. "Not soon enough," he stated.

CHAPTER 20

$\mathcal{T}$he following day Iris, accompanied by her new lady's maid, Becky, made their way to Hatchards book shop. The store had been a favorite of hers during her first Season, and she had wanted to visit it for several days. Being in London and not Cornwall meant that she would be able to read the latest books available and not wait months for them to be ordered or arrive.

The carriage rolled to a halt before the store, but not before she caught sight of Lady Sophie Hammilyn on the opposite side of the street, speaking with Lord Templedon.

Iris studied the pair, having not known they were acquainted. Well, certainly not as well acquainted as they appeared to be. Watching them, they looked to be friends indeed.

"Miss Bridges," she asked her maid, not wanting to use her given name just yet since they had only just commenced working together. "You worked in London for Lady Dellaware before her passing. Do you know much about society?"

Her maid, a woman past her prime but still young,

nodded eagerly. "Of course, Miss Cooper. I know most noble families in town."

Iris pointed out Lady Sophie and Lord Templedon on the street, hoping her new maid would know the pair as well. "Do you know how Lady Sophie is acquainted with Lord Templedon by chance?"

"I do, ma'am. They are distant cousins, several times removed. I believe they share the same great-grandmother."

"Really," Iris stated, watching the pair as they continued their conversation before moving off down the street. "I did not know that."

A footman opened the door, and Iris climbed down. Hatchards rose before her, the scent of leather filling her nostrils even outside the premises. How she had missed this store. More so than she missed balls and modistes. There was nothing quite like a story to sweep one off into a world so much brighter than one's own.

Except, she could no longer say such things. Not now that she had the duke. After last evening, the world paled a little in his presence. His touch, how wicked he was, and marvelous too. She had not known two people could do such things to each other.

It had made her wonder if it were possible for her to do the same to him. She had touched him once, and he seemed to enjoy her fondling. What would happen if her hand was replaced with her mouth, her tongue, just as he had performed?

As shiver stole through her, a heavy aching heat pooled in her belly.

Iris pushed the door to the store open, entering the shop filled with like-minded readers looking for their next great book. She walked about the store, debating what she felt like reading—poetry, romance, horror, so many to choose from.

A little while later, she found herself upstairs. Up in this part of the store, there were few people. Her maid stood beside the staircase, waiting patiently for her to return. Iris walked behind a bookcase, lost in contemplation, when a hand slipped about her waist and hauled her against a solid wall of muscle.

"You, my beautiful fianceé, are hard to find."

The deep, sensual baritone of her duke wrapped about her like a leather kid glove. She checked that no one was near them where they could be seen.

"Did you miss me then?" she asked, wrapping her arms about his neck, playing with the hair at his nape.

His hand slid up her back, pulling her closer. "I've missed you since the moment you left me hard and wanting in the carriage last evening. I came to find you this morning, and you were already gone. I'm most put out."

She chuckled, kissing him quickly. "Have I made it better? I'm sorry I was not at home."

The duke glanced about the shelves, reading some of the tomes at her back. "This is the philosophy section. Are you becoming a scientist?" he teased.

"No, of course not, but this section of the store also houses books on the stars and planets, which I do enjoy reading about."

"I do believe you reached the heavens last evening, my sweet." He grinned, his eyes alight with mischief.

She slapped at his shoulder. "You tease me. Do not be so cruel, or I shall not allow you to have me again in such a way."

He growled, letting her go and pulling her along the shelves. A door lay ajar just a little along, and Josh pulled her into the small room that looked to be one of the employee's offices. He shut the door behind him, snipping the lock.

Expectation thrummed through her, but she moved behind the desk, out of his reach. "You cannot touch me here,

Josh. There are customers about, and this is someone's desk. It would be rude of us to be inappropriate here."

He started around the desk, as slow as a fox after its prey. His darkened, hungry gaze made her shiver. "I like desks. I'm sure whoever owns this one would enjoy what I'm about to do to you on it if they had the chance."

Heat pooled between her legs, and she cursed her reactions to him, certainly here at least. She held out her hand, stilling him. "No, Josh. When you touch me, I cannot be silent. I'm mortified that your carriage driver now knows what you did to me last evening."

He chuckled, reaching for her. She wasn't quick enough to jump out of his scope, and he clasped the side of her dress, wrenching her against him.

"Your screams, your voice are what make men's lives worth living." He dipped his head, his lips trailing a line of fire down her neck, across her breasts, before he slipped the top of her gown down, exposing her to him.

She sighed, sliding her hand into his hair and clasping him to her as he teased her beaded flesh.

"You are too wicked for words," she gasped. He lifted his head and kissed her hard. His tongue tangled with hers. His mouth hungry and demanding. She met his every stroke, wanting him, no longer caring where they were or who could come upon them.

"I want to be wicked with you." His mouth took hers once again, and she lost all train of thought. Her wits spiraled, the emotions crashing through her strong and powerful.

"I want to be wicked with you too," she moaned when he pressed against her, where she ached most.

. . .

*J*osh was not sure what came over him when he'd arrived at his townhouse to find it empty of his betrothed and with the instructions from his mother that she was out shopping for books at Hatchards.

He'd left without a word, having thought of little else over the night but when he could see her next. He craved her. His body hungered for her presence, her touch, and sinful kisses.

It was utterly unfashionable he knew to be in lust with your wife, but that was exactly what he was. She may not be his just yet, but she would be soon, and then he doubted anyone could remove him from her side.

He kissed her deep and long, her hands exploring his body as much as his were hers. Her body drove him to distraction, her breasts the most perfect pair he'd ever beheld on a woman.

"Stop, Josh," she said, pushing at his chest with little effort.

Josh did as she asked. He met her gaze and did not miss the determined glint in her blue orbs. "You gave me so much pleasure last evening. I want to return the favor. You need to tell me what you like."

He swallowed, his cock spiking to attention. "Your hand on me," he said, taking her hand and guiding it to clasp him, "will do just now."

She squeezed him, stroking him through his buckskin breeches. Fuck, he wanted to come. He'd never been so fucking hard in his life.

"You kissed me where I did not think anyone ever kissed another." She licked her lips, eliciting a groan from him. "Am I able to kiss you there also? Would you like that?"

Would he like that? It took all of his self-control not to rip his front falls open and let her have at his cock. "It is possible, and I would love nothing more, but not until we're married. Hatchards is not the place for that."

She pouted, pushing him away from her. He frowned, wondering what she was doing.

"I want to do it now. Let me," she cooed, kneeling before him.

His breath came as fast as his heartbeat. He should stop her, make her listen to reason. Instead, he watched, fascinated, as she flipped open every button on his breeches. His cock jumped out, hard and long, weeping with the need of her.

Her eyes darkened with hunger, and he shut his a moment, fighting to control a situation he so obviously had lost control of. "It's so soft but hard, Josh. I want to lick it."

Christ, he was going to hell allowing this here. He also did not move, waited with bated breath for her to touch him. And then she did. At first running her finger along his length, following one of the engorged veins that ran from base to tip. Utterly fascinated and without a clue to what she was doing to him.

She was driving him to the point of madness. How had he lived without her for so long and believed himself to be content?

She bent over him, running her tongue along his cock, and he clasped the bookshelf at his back, holding himself upright. She lathed him with her tongue, teased his cock from base to tip. He groaned, wrapping his hands about her nape as she took him into her mouth, sucking him with an ability of a seasoned lover.

Josh worked into her mouth, her tongue slipping against him, her teeth with restraint. Iris gained momentum, cupping his balls with her hands, and he feared he would spend in her mouth.

He gasped, his balls drawing up tight. He wanted to come in her mouth, watch her swallow every ounce of him. But they were in a bookstore. People were but steps from them.

"Iris, stop, my darling. No more," he begged her, forcing her to release him. She stood, doing as he asked, and kissed him. Hard.

Josh lost all cohesive thought. All that mattered was Iris. That she was his and nothing would ever change that fact. He kissed her vigorously, tasting himself on her lips. "I do not think I shall survive the time we have left before you are mine. I ache for you."

She kneeled before him again, kissing his cock one more time. It jumped, pleased at her petting before she slipped the buttons back upon his front falls. "You will have to visit me more often at your townhouse, Your Grace. So we may get better acquainted before our marriage."

Josh helped Iris right her gown and pushed a wayward pin back into her long locks. "I will steal back into the townhouse as much as I can. Meet me in the library if you're able. I shall meet you there whenever I can. If not, I may steal into your room."

She grinned at his mischievous tone. "I'll see you tonight then," she said, her voice a siren's song to his blood. "After the Norwich ball."

He watched her walk from the small room, throwing him a wicked grin over her shoulder before she was gone. Josh slumped against the bookcase, his cock still hard and wanting attention.

He closed his eyes and breathed deep, forcing himself to calm his racing blood. Tonight was not too far away, at least. He would survive until then.

Perhaps.

CHAPTER 21

Sophie sipped her Madeira and studied Miss Cooper and the Dowager Duchess Penworth as they made a tour of the room, conversing with the others present at the Norwich ball. She ground her teeth, wondering what it was that Penworth saw in the little country mouse.

She was, in her esteemed opinion, no one of considerable beauty. Even with her rose-colored dress this evening, the heavier silk train that overlapped the gown at its back, Miss Cooper still was not the most handsome woman present.

Still, the duke sought her out, doted on her for some mysterious reason. She smiled to herself at what she had put into place earlier today. Her plan in getting what she wanted at any cost.

The duke would read the anonymous letter she had delivered to his Albany rooms, and he would be on guard this evening. It was the least that he deserved considering he had not offered to Sophie in all the time she had known her. He had given her hope where there was no hope to have. He would pay for treating her like a worthless piece of skirt he grew tired of and moved on from.

It was a pity that Miss Cooper would pay too for his deplorable actions toward her, but she would not apologize for seizing an opportunity that would make the duke regret his choice.

Poor man.

Sophie finished her drink, her attention snapping to the door when the duke was announced. His smile was fixed, but his eyes gave him away. Unease and speculation shone from his blue orbs, and she knew he had read her missive.

Good. The truth always came out to play eventually. It was time the duke owned up to his and face whatever came his way once spoken.

$\mathcal{T}$he Norwich ball was in full swing by the time the duchess and Iris arrived. They had dined first at home, deciding to forgo supper at the ball and return home then since the duchess had an early appointment in the morning with the modiste.

Iris looked about the room, trying to see if Josh had arrived when he was announced at the door. She drank in the sight of him as he paid his respects to the host and hostess before starting into the room.

He cut a line through the throng of guests, making his way over to them. Iris could not take her eyes from his person. His very presence made her heart jump, and she hoped that would always be the case.

What she felt around him, the utter thrill of having him at her side, bestowing sweet but equally wicked looks upon her, was an addiction for which she did not want a cure.

"Iris," he said, taking her hand. She expected him to kiss

her gloved fingers. Instead, he pulled her against him and kissed her cheek.

"You look beautiful, my darling. How I wish we were elsewhere."

His roguish words sent a thrill to spike through her. She heard some audible gasps but did not bother to look to see who had seen his familiarity. What was their affection to anyone else? They were to be married. There was nothing wrong with showing affection.

"I wish that too, Your Grace," she whispered before he stepped back and bowed to his mother, greeting her.

The duke stood beside her, taking a glass of wine from a passing footman. Iris watched as he studied the guests, a small frown between his brows.

"Is something troubling you, Your Grace?" she asked him, knowing that there was.

He shook his head, dismissing her concerns, but the way that he stood, as if on guard, ready to strike down any attack... His continued silence was at odds with his normal self.

Whatever was the matter with him?

"Ah, you are here this evening. So lovely to see you all," Lady Isolde Worthingham, now Duchess Moore said, joining them.

The dowager duchess kissed her daughter's cheek before reintroducing Her Grace to Iris.

"What a crush the Norwich ball is this evening. Do let me know if you wish to leave early, Mama. I'm more than happy to escort you and Miss Cooper home."

"Where is Moore this evening?" the dowager asked, glancing about the room and looking for her son-in-law.

"He did not wish to attend, and so I have come with Elizabeth. She is over near the smoking room talking to Lady Morrison."

Iris smiled as Lady Morrison gestured wildly as she spoke with Lady Elizabeth Worthingham, now Countess Muir before she noted Lord Templedon headed their way. Iris was reminded of seeing him on the street with Lady Sophie and couldn't help but wonder if his interest in her was borne out of Lady Sophie's interest in the duke.

Iris was no fool. Like so many young ladies present in London this Season, she knew Lady Sophie wanted to win the hand of the most-sought-after duke.

But would she continue to try to win him when Iris had won his hand already? If Lady Sophie attempted to injure her standing in society or ruin her engagement in some nefarious means, Iris doubted it would end in a marriage proposal from the duke. If anything, it would make him shy away from such an alliance with a woman so nasty at heart.

Lord Templedon bowed, greeting them all affably. Josh placed her hand upon his arm, marking her as his without a word spoken.

"How jolly this ball is this evening. I was hoping to make it even grander by stealing away your betrothed, Your Grace?" he asked the duke, his eyes calculating but amused.

Iris did not trust him in the least, not after seeing him with Lady Sophie, but still, what could the man say or do that would persuade her to break off her engagement to the duke? Their alliance may not be born out of love, he had kissed her, and they had been caught. Nothing more than that. But that did not mean their union could not grow into love and adoration. Something she was hoping was already happening between them.

As for Templedon's offer to dance, there was no harm in it. He could not injure her in any way. Iris let go of the duke's arm and reached for Templedon. "Of course, my lord. I shall like to dance."

She cast a lingering glance at His Grace as she walked out

onto the floor, not missing the deadly glare he had marked against his lordship.

Why was it that Josh hated the man so very much? He may be a rogue, calculating and teasing toward the opposite sex, but he was as dangerous as a mouse to Iris.

No one compared to Josh, and she knew no one ever would.

"I discovered the oddest thing the other day, my lord," Iris said as they lined up for a country reel.

"Really?" he queried, throwing her a benign smile. "Do tell me what you discovered. I'm always up for a good intrigue."

The musicians started to play, and the dance commenced. Iris moved and weaved about Lord Templedon, pleased that this dance at least allowed some conversation.

"I saw you on Piccadilly street the other day with Lady Sophie. I did not know that you were, in fact, cousins."

The smile on his lordship slipped a little at her words before he righted his countenance and was once more himself. Iris thought about that little slip. Whatever did it mean? Guilty conscience, perhaps?

"Distant cousins, Miss Cooper, but we are friends. We're family, after all. Blood must come before anything else and all that. Do you not agree?"

Iris could agree with that statement, of course. But did his blood kin to Lady Sophie mean they were in cohorts together to injure Iris in some way? Steal the duke from her?

She wasn't sure why she had this inkling, but the fact Lady Sophie had not reached out the hand of friendship since her betrothal announcement did make her question. Lady Sophie had wanted to be friends before, so why not after?

Was it because she wanted the duke for herself?

"Of course, that goes without saying," she said. "Please give my regards to Lady Sophie when you speak with her next and tell her I miss our chats. I thought we were becoming fine friends, but I have not spoken to her for several days now, not even when we attend the same balls. I hope I have not offended her in some way."

Iris watched Lord Templedon. He glanced about the room, a fine sheen of sweat on his brow. "Of course not. I'm certain it is nothing but a coincidence that you have not conversed. I shall mention it to her. Ensure she calls on you soon."

Iris smiled, no longer caring if the friendship continued or not. She merely wanted both Templedon and Lady Sophie to know she had seen them, and her curiosity was spiked. "That would be most appreciated," she said, moving down the line of dancers, taking her from his lordship a moment before the dance brought her back again.

"Speaking of spying, I did see you as well out the other day, riding with the duke in Hyde Park. I did not think you would go there since, well, you know," he alluded, his eyes sparkling with malice. "It was where your accident occurred. I thought it quite harsh of His Grace to be so ignorant of your pain."

Spy? She had never spied on him as he was suggesting with his words. She had merely arrived at the bookstore and seen them. "That was a long time ago, my lord. I prefer to move forward in my life. I know Redgrove would wish that for me."

"Of course," he agreed. "You know, of course, that Redgrove was an acquaintance of mine and the duke's. I only say this because I care for your emotional well-being. It must have been hard to lose your betrothed in such a foolish manner."

Iris frowned, uncertain of what he meant. "Redgrove took a turn too fast. There was no foolishness in his mistake. He made an error and paid dearly for it. We both did. But he was not acting the fool."

"Hmm, of course, Miss Cooper," he stated, disbelief written across his features as clear as a Cornwall night sky. What was the man trying to allude to? Did he know something that she did not of the accident?

The dance came to an end, and before she could ask, Lord Templedon had deposited her back with Josh and his mother. His sister having moved on to other acquaintances of theirs.

Josh placed her arm on his, holding her close. "I do not like you dancing with that rogue. He's not to be trusted."

She smiled at her fiancé, enjoying his public display of jealousy. "Templedon is no threat to you, Your Grace. No one is," she admitted, no truer words spoken.

His eyes darkened with promise, and Iris counted down the hours until she was abed and Josh could sneak in to see her. Would he come tonight? Was he game enough to steal upstairs and into her room?

Iris crossed her fingers, hoping her wish would come true and the ball passed quickly so they could leave.

CHAPTER 22

They returned to the house on Hanover Square in the early hours of the morning. The duchess had left them in the parlor downstairs after they had enjoyed a cup of tea before retiring for the night.

"I should let you rest," the duke said. He sat beside her, the dark shadows under his eyes telling Iris that he was as tired as they were. The Season was so busy, with endless late nights. It was not surprising that he would not be able to sneak into her room this morning.

"I understand. You should go and gain some yourself." Iris reached out, running her hand across his stubbled jaw. His beard tickled her palm. "I cannot wait until I have you beside me every night and morning. What fun we shall have then."

The duke chuckled, half-groaned before laying his head back against the settee. "I do not want to leave you. I would join you upstairs still, even with the house servants starting to go about their duties, but I will not have your reputation sullied. I will protect you at all costs. Even the cost to my ease since I want you so very much."

She leaned against him, laying her head upon his shoulder. "How much do you want me, Your Grace?" It could not be any more than she wanted him. The days stretched endlessly being without him. She wanted to be married to the duke and now. Not in three weeks.

He picked up her fingers and laid them against his falls. "I want you quite a lot. Do you not see?"

Iris stroked him through his satin knee-breeches. He hardened further in her hand, and heat spiked through her, circling down to her core. "When will I see you again?" she asked, not halting her teasing.

He covered her hand with his, increasing the tension. Iris crossed her legs, need pooling between her thighs. How she wanted him. This madness he had created in her was endless.

"Tonight. There is the Russell musical this evening. Cry off, say you have a headache, your courses, anything. I shall join you after eleven. My mother will be out by then and will not return for several hours."

Iris smiled, unable to count down the hours until she saw him again. She moved closer still and kissed him, touched and teased him as their mouths fused. His tongue tangled with hers, and she didn't want to wait until tonight. The man drove her to distraction.

He clasped her face, their kiss turning into a firestorm of need. Josh eased her back on the settee, coming over her. Their hands were everywhere, touching, petting, teasing until she could not take any more.

The cool morning air prickled against her legs as Josh slid her gown up about her waist, exposing her to him. He ripped his front falls open, his cock springing engorged and eager between them. Her face must have given away her thoughts.

"I will not take you here and now, but I will make you come." His thick, guttural voice made her insides clench, and she nodded, letting him do what he wished.

He could do anything to her right at this moment, and

Iris did not think she'd say a word to stop him so long as he made her feel the pleasure she had last in his arms.

*J*osh glanced at the door, sitting slightly ajar. The servants could enter at any moment, or his mother if she were to do one final check on them before retiring.

None of that mattered. He had to have her. Well, as much as he could have her without actually taking her virginity. Josh pushed his cock against her wet, hot flesh. He moaned her name, running himself along her slick heat. Her eyes closed in pleasure, her legs lifting up about his hips and holding him against her.

He would spend on her. That was a certainty. The rioting, vigorous emotions, and the care he felt for the woman in his arms were new. She would be his soon, and they could do whatever they wanted whenever they pleased. No rules, no scandal could touch them then.

The word love reverberated about in his mind like a whistle.

He had never loved anyone. Not truly loved the way a man loved a woman. Something told Josh that what he felt for the woman in his arms was not common. It was not something that one dispensed with or took for granted.

She ground against him, pushing up and taking what she wanted. He lost his breath, his balls pulling tight. His release was imminent, and he bit the inside of his mouth, forcing himself to hold off, to wait until she shattered in his arms.

Iris clasped the lapels of his jacket, pulling him against her for a kiss, and he kissed away her scream as she climaxed against his cock, spiking his own pleasure.

He spent upon her mons and stomach with an orgasm that seemed to go on forever. If only that were so.

Being that they were in the parlor where anyone could come upon them, the morning light breaking through the heavy velvet blinds told him he was running out of time.

Josh untied his cravat and helped clean up Iris as best as he could. The little siren lay on the settee, watching him as he wiped away his seed, seemingly unfazed by the fact they were dancing with scandal.

He adored her all the more for her fortitude.

"Come, you had best leave for your room," he said, buttoning himself up and checking his attire before he left the parlor.

She sighed, but instead of leaving, draped her arms over his shoulders, her eyes sparkling with pleasure. "I shall see you this evening, Your Grace," she whispered, kissing him quickly before turning on her heel and leaving him watching after her.

He clasped his stomach, his body rejecting the fact she was leaving him and that it would be several hours before he saw her again. Damn the rules of etiquette and their antiquated expectations for men and women.

He waited a suitable amount of time and then left via the back door, walking past the mews so no one would see him going a considerable amount of time after he had delivered his mother and betrothed home.

As he walked the short distance to his bachelor rooms, his stomach churned at the reminder of the missive he had received just before last evening's ball. The veiled threat the copy of his bet at Whites all those years ago meant.

Who had sent him his words, copied down to appear the same as the original page in the betting book he did not know. He suspected Templedon, but to steal such a thing from Whites would mean suspension.

Would he do such a thing? Templedon enjoyed his club. Or was someone else behind the threat? That he supposed he ought to find out or tell Iris of his wrongdoing before she heard it from an individual not himself.

She would never forgive him if she knew the truth, his cowardice in not owning up to his wrong. Nor would she marry him.

All facts he could not bear the thought of. Not now that she was his in all but name, his heart, body, and soul. Now and forever.

CHAPTER 23

*L*ater that afternoon, Iris stepped into Gunter's Tea Shop on Berkeley Square and joined Lady Elizabeth Worthingham, Countess Muir for afternoon tea.

She sat midway in the shop and waved to Lady Muir when she entered the store. The countess started for her. Bussing both her cheeks in welcome, she said, "Miss Cooper, I'm sorry I'm running a little late. The traffic today was unmentionable."

Iris waved her concerns aside, happy to get to know Josh's sister and his family a little more. "Thank you for inviting me here. I have not been in Gunter's for some years. Not since my first Season, I believe."

"Really?" Her ladyship glanced about the room, catching the eye of an employee who started their way to serve them. "I come here all the time. The ices and sorbets are to die for."

Iris chuckled. "I will be sure to order them then."

"You should," Lady Muir said, studying her a moment. "I must say how happy I am that our darling little brother has finally found his heart. We were starting to worry he would never marry and forever be about our skirts."

Iris ignored her belief that Josh was marrying her because of love. No matter how much she longed that was the case, it was not. He did like her very much, and for now, that would have to do. Especially considering they had been caught in the throes of passion by his mother, and marriage was not negotiable.

Her mind conjured up this morning in the parlor and the exquisite pleasure he had wrought upon her body. She could only imagine and dream of what it would be like when they were together in the truest sense. What he would feel like within her, pushing her toward the type of release she already experienced in his hands, by his mouth and manhood.

Heat kissed her cheeks, and she sipped the lemonade placed before her.

"I am very happy," she admitted, and she was. More than she ever hoped to be, considering their betrothal was not the usual kind. Not that others needed to know such things. "The wedding plans are coming along well, and I believe the dowager duchess has everything in hand."

Lady Muir chuckled. "I have little doubt that Mama does." Her ladyship smiled. "Will you allow me to call you Iris? You may call me Elizabeth in return. We're to be family, after all. No need to stand on ceremony."

The hand of friendship, the kindness this family bestowed on Iris. She could not believe her fortune. "I would love it if you called me Iris. Thank you."

Elizabeth shook her head, spooning pink sorbet into her mouth. "I will admit I was concerned when Mama said she was sponsoring her friend's daughter, but after meeting you, I think it has been the loveliest gift to my mother all year. She misses us all now that we're married and settled else-where. I'm glad that you will be with Josh and Mama not too far away in the dowager house. When you have children, she will be kept younger still by having a purpose again. Helping you to raise your children. The ducal line."

"I hope we are able to have children, a son especially." The idea of a little Josh running about her skirts, rolling down green embankments of grass before the great Dunsleigh estate, made her long for things to come.

"Is it difficult having been in love before? I have only been blessed once with the emotion. I'm happy for you that you were able to find it a second time with my brother."

Elizabeth asked the question with no malice in her tone, and Iris thought about how to answer her. Her life now was so different from how it had been when engaged to Redgrove. She was younger, without any injuries impacting her life then. All her thoughts had been on marrying her first Season and not her second. No one wanted to be a wallflower. Redgrove had offered, he was polite and handsome, and she had said yes. She was no longer so agreeable. With the duke, everything was so different, but in a better way. More delicious and intense kind of way.

"While I cared for Redgrove, to my shame, I did not love him. We were friends and went along well enough together, but it was not a love match."

"Not like it is with my brother. How happy I am for you, dear," Elizabeth said, reaching out and patting her hand.

Love match? The statement startled her. Her union with the duke wasn't a love match either. Well, on the duke's behalf, it was not. Iris thought about the emotion, the kaleidoscope of feelings that bombarded her each time she was around His Grace.

Was she in love?

Had she fallen in love with her betrothed?

Surely not, and yet… Panic assailed her that Lady Muir may be correct. No, not maybe correct, was correct.

She loved him.

Elizabeth's mouth twisted into a knowing smile. "You did not realize, did you, Iris?" She picked up her tea, taking a sip. "It is obvious to those who share the emotion to recognize it in those about us, just as it is easy to spy a marriage that is not a happy union. I believe, and even if my brother has not spoken the words, he is in love with you also. It is as plain as day."

Elizabeth's words sent a thrill through her. Did Josh love her also? She clasped her stomach, her tummy roiling in glee. "Do you truly believe that?"

"Of course," Elizabeth said without hesitation. "He hangs about your skirts more than he used to hang around Mama's when he was a boy."

Iris chuckled at the visualization the words brought forth before Elizabeth continued. "I've never known him to be at home so often during the Season, and as for when you are at balls and parties, he does not like you dancing with others and takes every opportunity to be at your side."

But was that love? Iris knew they certainly lusted after each other but had they fallen for each other somehow in the middle of their hasty engagement?

"How do you know he does not like me dancing with other men?" Iris queried.

"I suggest you glance at your betrothed when you are next in the arms of another gentleman, and you shall see for yourself how put out he is when you leave him for another."

Iris nodded, determined to do that the next time they were out. How wonderful it would be that her husband did indeed love her. She had not thought to make a love match, and so to hear that the possibility that Josh loved her soothed any trepidations she had at marrying a duke.

"I will take notice, but he has not said anything to me. Do gentlemen usually state such a thing to their wives before or after marriage? Would it be unfashionable and crass to say it first?"

"Bless your sweet heart," Elizabeth stated, smiling. "If you feel what I suspect you do for my brother, there is no reason why a woman cannot take control of her life and speak the truth. Whatever will come of that declaration. But," she added, pushing away her now empty cup of sorbet, "I think you shall find the duke receptive of your words and will find they are returned in all haste."

*L*ater that night, Iris lay in bed, having fibbed to the duchess that she had a headache, using the excuse of too much sugar from Gunter's Tea Shop that afternoon. She had been put to bed, and Iris made sure she had dismissed her maid for the night, just in case Josh did do as he said he would and sneak into her suite of rooms.

She dozed on and off, the idea that she loved the duke not quite real to her. She had not seen him all day, and she had certainly missed his company, but that did not mean she loved him.

Light footsteps sounded in the passage before the handle on her door turned, and a dark figure entered her room, snipping the lock behind them.

"Miss me, my darling?"

The deep, recognizable baritone rolled over her like a wave, and she knew the truth of her situation. She loved him. She loved the Duke of Penworth.

"Of course," she whispered back as he came into view. He kneeled on the bed, crawling up over her. She chuckled, reaching for him. He was so warm, masculine, and hers—all hers to do with as she pleased for the rest of her life.

She could not be so fortunate. How had she been so blessed?

"I missed you too," he admitted, taking her lips and pulling her into a dance of desire. Iris kissed him back with all that she felt for the man in her arms. The love, the pride, his sweetness, and care. She threaded her fingers into his hair, pulling him closer still, wanting him with a need that surpassed all considerations.

They would be married soon, in under three weeks. It could not hurt if she gave herself to him, body and soul.

She pushed off his jacket, baring him to his shirt. Josh kneeled, ripping it out of his breeches and throwing it into a darkened corner of the room.

Iris untied the small ribbons at her bust, wanting her shift off, to be skin on skin, completely naked with him. His eyes darkened with understanding, and he paused, his breaths coming in short, fast spurts.

"We should not do this, Iris. It is wrong, and I promised myself I would not ruin you."

Iris sat up, wiggling on the bed to release the shift from under her before she pulled it from her body, throwing it in the direction Josh's shirt had flown. The night air kissed her skin, her nipples beaded, and she shivered at the hunger burning in Josh's eyes.

A muscle worked at his jaw, his hands fisted at his sides. She reached for him, taking one fist and opening it, laying it against the sensitive flesh of her breast. "You will not ruin me. We're to be married. There is no shame in what we are doing. Two consenting adults who are promised to each other and who want the same."

His hand kneaded her breast, his thumb and finger rolling her nipple between their pads. She closed her eyes, sensation spiking between her legs.

"Are you sure?" he asked again, coming over her and settling between her legs. His manhood jutted against her sensitive skin, and she gasped, wrapping her legs about his hips.

How she wanted him, ached for him to fill her, to take her. She undulated against his cock, and he gasped, clasping her hands and pinning them above her head.

"You're a minx. Do you know what you do to me?"

She tried to place him near her core a second time, teasing herself as much as she taunted him. "I presume it is similar to what I feel now."

"And what do you feel?" he asked, pushing himself the smallest amount into her.

Iris gasped, clasping his hands tight as he continued to hold her down. Oddly, the position did not scare her. It merely made her want him all the more. See what else he had in store for her.

"Need. I need you, Josh," she admitted.

He took her lips quickly before letting go of one of her hands to guide himself into her. The sensation of his manhood stretching her for the first time was odd but not painful. Certainly nothing like she had been led to believe by her mama.

Oh no, there was no pain from the need that thrummed through her and drove her to distraction. Impatient, Iris pulled him closer with her legs. He groaned as he settled himself fully against her, holding her down.

She bit her lip, wondering when he would move. She would expire if he did not do something!

And then he did shift, rocked into her, slow, delicious thrusts that allowed her body to adjust to this new intrusion. He needn't be so innocent. She wanted him, all of him, to feel and revel in the lovemaking of her future husband.

He kissed her hard, taking her with a relentlessness that left her gasping for breath. He let go of her hands, and she clasped his back, fighting for footing. Each time he took her,

her body, hungry with need, wanted more. Her body did not feel like itself. Every nerve tingled, her core wet and aching. Iris moaned, whimpered his name, and still, it was not enough. She doubted it would ever be so.

*J*osh rolled onto his back, taking Iris with him. He fought for breath to stem the need to spend in her tight, wet heat too soon. She would come, shatter upon him, or he would die trying.

She sat atop him, her eyes wide at the new position, but she did not move. "Your turn to fuck me, Iris darling," he said crudely.

She adjusted herself on him, and he groaned The action made his balls tighten. "How? What am I to do up here?" she asked him.

He clasped her hips, urging her up and down. She followed his lead, doing as he showed her.

"Oh yes, I see now," she breathed, taking over from his instruction and seeking pleasure for herself. She was magnificent above him, rocking on his cock, taking him deep and hard. He breathed deep, stemming his release. So beautiful. He reached up, cupping her breast, teasing her beaded nipple.

She threw her head back, his name a chant on her lips. Holy fuck, he had not thought making love with her would be so utterly satisfying. It was better than a benign ideal. She was beyond his expectations, his hopes, in all ways.

And she was his.

Forever. Not just this night, but for a lifetime.

How had he been so lucky? So fortunate.

She tightened about him, and he knew she was close, and then she shattered. She threw back her head, her long, dark locks a waterfall down her back and over her shoulders. Her beauty took his breath away, and he came, hard and long in her cunny.

He remembered to breathe, watched her with a fascination he'd never had before as she rocked atop him, slowly returning to him and away from her climax. Milking him of his seed and every ounce of pleasure he gave her.

Her hands ran over his chest, a lopsided, satisfied grin on her lips.

"I hope you enjoyed yourself, my darling wife-to-be."

She sighed, coming to rest in the crook of his arm. She lay one leg over his, holding him close. "So, will it always be like that between us? I should think married couples never venture outside their homes if that is the case."

He laughed, reaching down and pulling the bedding over them both, not wanting her to catch a chill. "I will endeavor for it to be so. I want nothing but the best for you, my darling. Not just here when we're alone, but in all things in life. I never want to see you disappointed."

"You could never disappoint me," she said, clasping his jaw.

Josh fought down the guilt that rose at her words. He had never disappointed her yet, but should she find out the truth, or he told her the truth of her past that involved him, she would never look at him the same again.

And he needed to tell her what happened before whoever it was that had sent him the missive of the Whites bet beat him to it.

"I hope I do not," he admitted, holding her closer still. *Or if I do, that you will forgive me my sins.*

CHAPTER 24

"They are still engaged, so my letter to the duke has not worked," Sophie seethed to Lord Templedon, who stood beside her at the Battenlodge ball. Penworth waltzed past her with his betrothed, the cripple whom he gazed upon as if the sun itself shone from her very core, warming and lighting up those around her.

Miss Iris Cooper. The attraction the duke had with his betrothed was beyond Sophie's comprehension. It simply did not make sense. He ought to be with a woman such as herself. Not some penniless cripple from Cornwall.

Whoever heard of such an absurd notion.

"I should think they are still on amicable terms because he has not told her the truth of that day that he was there. Had placed the bet in Whites that Redgrove took upon himself to better."

"Then I will have to tell her myself," she stated, more than willing to do as she threatened. Of course, if it meant that she married Josh Worthington herself, she would do anything.

Templedon threw her a disbelieving look. "If you do that, and he becomes aware of your interference, he will never marry you. He will punish you and anyone who came between him and his betrothed. Not that I think anyone will. The duke is smitten. Look at him." Templedon gestured just as the happy couple waltzed past a second time.

Sophie felt her eye twitch. "Should we injure Miss Cooper? Make the duke see her for the weakling she is? If she is injured and needs a cane to walk, he would surely not want to pollute his bloodline with so feeble a person."

Templedon gaped, and she sighed, supposing being so cruel was taking the matter a little too far.

"You would never do such a thing. Miss Cooper may not be as fine a catch as you would be, but she is who he chooses, and she's a sweet woman. I can see the attraction."

Sophie slapped at his arm, disliking his words. "Do not jest. This is beyond a time for joking about."

Templedon sighed. "I have hinted that there is more to that day than what Miss Cooper knows, but so far, she has not asked outright. I fear if I say any more, she will think me morbid, having always brought up the death of Redgrove."

Sophie pursed her lips, her mind a whirl of thoughts. "I suppose you are right. We shall have to come at her from a different angle. Or perhaps, we tell her the truth in an anonymous letter and let fate decide my future. If they quarrel or are out of sorts at an event after I have sent the missive, I shall make my move then. I will make the duke see me instead of that imbecile Miss Cooper."

"How do you intend to make him see you when he hasn't looked at you all Season? Even before Miss Cooper came to town."

She rolled her eyes. Really, men were at times the stupidest sex. "I'm a woman, and I have my wiles. If I can get him to myself at a ball, I'm certain he will seek my comfort, which I will be more than willing to give him to mend his broken heart."

"Do not ruin yourself in the process, Sophie. Society will not forgive you."

She shrugged, knowing she would not. Instead, she would gain her duke, and by foul means or none. He would bend to her will, and he would turn away from Miss Cooper, whom he should never have considered in the first place.

*T*he last few weeks before their wedding passed in a blur. They dined out at friends' and family estates, afternoons at the opera, and nights of pleasure. Then, just yesterday, they received word that Lady Victoria, now Marchioness Melvin, would be traveling back from Paris to attend the wedding. Lady Alice Worthingham, Viscountess Arndel too would be there, which had the dowager duchess excited beyond measure to have all her children in one place, even if it was only for a day.

Iris, too, had her parents' arrival to look forward to. They were expected first among the guests and would be in London by the end of the week.

She stood in the modiste on Saville Road, holding herself as still as she could as they pinned the hem of her blue silk wedding gown to an appropriate height.

The gown was such a light shade of blue it almost looked white, the bodice silk brocade while the skirt was of fine chiffon, layered extensively to ensure her modesty was retained. The gown reminded Iris of a Roman lady's silk tunic, ethereal and flattering to her figure. She hoped Josh admired her dress.

"How beautiful you will be, Iris darling. If I have not told you already, your marriage to my son warms my heart."

The dowager's words were welcome and heartfelt. Iris leaned down, pulling her into a quick embrace. "It is I who is fortunate." She turned back to look in the mirror, not quite believing the country-born-and-raised woman from Cornwall, a woman who could not be more different to those in the social circle she now socialized in, was marrying a duke. And not just any titled gentleman whom on paper filled all her requirements, but a marriage of affection.

Of perhaps even love.

Iris no longer questioned her feelings for the duke. They were solid and unmovable. She loved him. Every ounce of his being. But did he love her? That she did not know. "How is it that the wedding is next week? This month has been a marvelous whir of entertainment and gaiety."

"There are more to be had," the duchess stated, seating herself on a nearby settee. "His Grace has declared you will remain in town, so I shall have a little while longer with you both before we return to Dunsleigh."

"Your alterations are complete, Miss Cooper," the modiste said, packing away her pins. "Shall I help you to change?"

"Thank you, yes," she said, going over to a little private section of the store that ensured privacy and switched back into her morning gown. Iris stood while the modiste unbuttoned her dress before stepping out of it. Her toe caught on the fine material, and before she could catch herself, Iris fell, landing hard on her injured hip.

Pain shot through her thigh, and she was unable to stop the yelp that escaped. The duchess was there in a moment, helping her to sit, checking her for injuries.

"I am well. I merely tripped on my dress."

"Oh, Miss Cooper. I'm so sorry. It is my fault, entirely. Please forgive me," the modiste lamented, her eyes fearful.

Iris patted the modiste's hand. "It is my fault. I can be a little inefficient at times."

"Here, my dear. Let me help you up."

Iris took the duchess's hand. On two feet again, her head spun as a sharp pain shot through her leg. She had been so careful not to aggravate her injury. There was little doubt in her mind that it would pain her for several days. Not that she cared, she was used to her leg being counterproductive, but she did not want to limp down the aisle toward Josh.

"Thank you," she said, rubbing her leg as the modiste fetched her morning dress before slipping it over her head. "Would you mind, Your Grace, if we returned home? I would like to rest for a time. We have the Lowes ball this evening, and I do not want to miss it."

"Of course, dear. You need not ever ask."

They returned home to Hanover Square, and Iris excused herself after ordering a bath. A long, hot soak was what her leg required. It would soothe the muscles and help ease her pain. That the duchess had ordered a tisane too would be welcome. She would attend the ball this evening with her betrothed, as promised.

osh arrived just before lunch, wanting to take Iris out for a carriage ride. He entered the front downstairs parlor and found his mama having her lunch alone, no sign of his betrothed.

"Good day, Mother," he said, bending to kiss her in welcome. "I came to invite Iris out for a ride, but I see she is already out."

His mother placed down her small sandwich, shaking her head. "Oh no, dearest. Iris is home. She is, however, unfortunately unavailable. She is upstairs bathing. There was a mishap a short time ago at the modiste, and she injured herself."

Josh frowned, and his mother waved at him to sit. "I do not wish to alarm you. Iris is well. She tripped on her gown and landed heavily on her leg. A bath will soon put her to rights, make her comfortable. She's determined to accompany you to the Lowes ball this evening. I do not know why she is so firm on attending. Do you know, my dear?" his mother asked, picking up her cup of tea and watching him over the rim as she took a sip.

He thought on the question a moment before the answer came to him. "There are to be fireworks. Their estate abuts the Thames, and Lord and Lady Lowes will host them there. Iris, I have found, enjoys fireworks. I do not believe she has seen many in her life."

"Oh, well, that explains her eagerness," the duchess stated. "Would you care to join me? I can have more sandwiches brought in. They really are delicious. Cook has placed ham and cheese in the middle of the bread. Quite marvelous in fact."

Josh chuckled, standing and starting for the door. "I cannot today, Mother. I shall return this evening to collect you both for the ball," he said, waving to his parent and starting for the front door, except, coming out into the foyer, he noted no one about. Doing a quick turn, he took the stairs two at a time, striding in the direction of Iris's room before anyone saw him.

Thankfully Iris's room was in the same wing of the house as his, so he could always lie and say he was collecting paperwork from his quarters.

Her door was closed, and he stood at the threshold, hearing the splashing of water within.

Was she bathing still?

He entered, glad to find her bedroom empty of her lady's maid. He locked the door, starting for the closet and where the small private bathroom was located. He leaned against the doorframe, watching as she lathed her arms with soap, the scent of lavender rising with the steam coming off the water.

She looked utterly delightful and comfortable. He was

glad of it. The last thing he wanted was for her to be in pain. "Are you well, my darling? I heard you had a fall."

She jumped, turning to look at him over her shoulder. Her welcoming smile made his heart jump in his chest. Josh went to her, kneeling beside the tub and taking her hand. "What happened? Is there anything that I can do to make you more comfortable?"

"I tripped, that is all. The bath and tisane your mama had sent up has helped. I shall keep myself warm for the remainder of the day."

"If you are unable to attend the ball, we can spend the night here. I would prefer to have you to myself in any case."

She reached out, clasping his cheek. He took the opportunity to kiss her. She was so beautiful it made his body ache. "I believe these are the last fireworks this Season, and I so wish to see them. Please say that we can go. Not," she continued, smiling mischievously, "that I do not love having you all to myself. For I do, and after next week, we will no longer have to be separated if we do not want to be."

"Mmm, I shall enjoy that perk of our marriage, among other things," he teased her. "Shall I fetch you your drying cloth? Do you wish to dress?"

She threw him a disbelieving look. "Really, Your Grace? Anyone would think that you wanted to see your fianceé naked. As it is, you should not be in here."

"It is my house. I can go anywhere I please," he teased, knowing that was far from the truth.

She chuckled. "You and I both know that is not valid. She stood without help, and before he could offer a hand. Josh stared up at her, an Amazonian goddess, and he, her servant. He reached out, circling her injured thigh with his hand. "I wish I could take away your pain."

Goosebumps rose on her skin, and he remembered himself, going to get her towel quickly. "You make me forget myself." He helped her out of the bath. She wrapped herself in the towel, watching him. "You make me forget myself too."

A shiver stole down his spine. The emotions whirling in his body, through his heart, were not normal. He felt so much more when around her. He'd never felt for anyone what he felt for the woman standing before him, his future duchess.

"As much as I would like to stay, it is better that I do not. I will return this evening to accompany you to the ball. Wear a cloak over your gown. It will be cooler in the gardens and by the water."

She nodded, her eyes bright with expectation. Josh took the opportunity to kiss her. The kiss was hard, demanding, and short. He left her, his breathing as ragged as her own, and started down the passage. The night already too many hours away.

CHAPTER 25

"Why are we at the embankment, Your Grace?" Iris asked Josh as the carriage rolled to a halt some distance from where they were supposed to be heading. The Lowes ball.

Josh grinned, helping her alight and walking them down a small gravel path before they came to steps leading down to a stationary boat on the Thames. "We are not attending the ball this evening, my dear. I have something else planned for you."

"Really?" Iris smiled at the knowing look on the duke's visage. What on earth had he planned? "Was this the reason your mama cried off accompanying us, and I had to take my maid?"

"It is," he stated. They walked the short distance to the stairs before Josh helped her down the few stone steps. There was a boat moored at the small wooden dock. It was only a small vessel, occupied by a singular man at the rear of the boat, a seat that sat under a wooden awning, screening those from paddling them along. "Where will Miss Bridges sit?" she asked as Josh helped her onto the vessel.

"In the carriage." He threw her a mischievous wink before joining her. They settled on the many cushions and blankets before they were soon paddling out onto the Thames, the current pulling them out in the direction of the ocean.

Iris looked out at London that sparked with light on either side of the river. The sounds of the city met her ears, of shouts and laughter, music and industrial dins—the soothing lap of water against the side of the boat. "I've never been on a boat before," she admitted, wondering if this would be the time to tell Josh that she also could not swim.

The boat slowed but stayed a little out on the water, away from the water's edge. On this part of the river, grand London homes lined the banks, and then, unexpectedly, a high-pitched squeal sounded before light burst to life into the night sky above them.

"You brought me to the fireworks?" she gasped, looking at him quickly before the next firework burst into a million stars above them.

"I wanted you all to myself when we watched them. I could not hold you as I do now had we been in the gardens at Lowes ball."

Iris's heart did a little flip. No one had ever been so sweet, so adoring and accommodating to her in her life. She tore her gaze from the fireworks and met Josh's eyes. His burned with emotion, one she now hoped he was brave enough to admit to.

"I love your gift just as I love you," she said, praying she was not wrong in what she believed he felt for her too.

He pulled her closer still, cradling her face in his hands. "I'm so pleased you said those words, Iris, as I have utterly and completely fallen in love with you too."

Tears burned in her eyes, and she blinked, trying to stem the rioting emotions within her. "You do?" she queried, needing to hear his declaration again and again, so she knew it to be true.

"I've never felt with anyone the way I feel when I'm around you." He kissed the tip of her nose just as another burst of color scattered across the night sky. "You must know, you must have sensed that I am nonsensical when around you. You are my heart, and when we marry next week, I never wish to be parted from you."

There was no stopping the tears this time. Iris fumbled for her handkerchief, but always there for her, Josh held out his for her use. She dabbed at her cheeks.

He loved her, and she loved him. How lucky that he had kissed her that night and the duchess had caught them. To think of him courting another was unfathomable now. The duke was hers, and she would love him forever.

"A week seems too long to wait, but then we will have a lifetime together, so I suppose I shall be patient."

Josh chuckled, leaning down to reach into a small picnic basket that Iris had not noticed before. He pulled out two glass flutes, handing them to her before taking out the champagne.

Popping the bottle, he poured them both a glass. "After your fall today, and the pain that you suffered, I did not think a ball was in your best interest, but I also did not want you to miss the fireworks you've grown so fond of."

"And so you thought to hire a boat and take me out onto the Thames at night to view them together. A romantic cruise just the two of us."

His smile warmed her. "That is exactly what I thought. Have I succeeded?"

Iris tapped her glass against his, downing her champagne before reaching for him. "I think you have succeeded very well indeed, Your Grace. I am very well pleased."

. . .

*J*osh tipped his champagne out into the Thames before dropping the glass into the many cushions and blankets they lay upon. He took Iris into his arms, kissing her hard and long. He lost himself in the feel of her. Her sweetness and favorable response to his kisses.

He would never tire of having her so.

More fireworks crackled across the night sky. They glanced up, lost to the beauty of the entertainment for a moment. They cruised the river for a time after the fireworks had ended. The picnic basket held bread and cheese, a little ham, and chicken. They drank champagne and nibbled on the feast, talking of the wedding, of what they wished to do after being married.

"How soon would you like children?" she asked him before popping another slice of cheese between her lips.

"We're young, and I would like you all to myself for a time. A year or two," he answered, happy to allow her to decide when she was ready. Even in this decision, he mused, he would allow her to determine their fate.

His lips twitched at how different his life now was after meeting Iris. He no longer thought of other women, of who his mistress would be should he take one on. His club had lost some of its charms since women were not allowed. Had Josh thought that such a change could occur in his life, he would have scoffed at the notion only a month ago.

How odd and wonderful that life could change so quickly and for the better.

"I've always wanted children, so I think a year and no more." Iris sipped her champagne, wagging the glass flute before him when she emptied it. He chuckled, pouring her some more. "Thank you," she said, pausing. "I've never been to Dunsleigh. Is it beautiful?"

"Beautiful? The word is too innocuous to describe your future home. Dunsleigh is magnificent. Grand and opulent, welcoming and warm. The grounds are lovely and the staff too. Everyone there will love you, Iris. Just as their duke and master also does."

A blush stole over her cheeks. How utterly charming his future wife was.

"I know the estate is large, and I shall ensure I learn all there is to know so as not to disappoint anyone."

He reached out, picking up her gloved hand and kissing her fingers. "You will not disappoint anyone. You are an intelligent, capable woman. I have no reservations regarding your ability."

They rowed ever closer to the dock, and Josh could see one of his servants waiting for them. He sighed, not wanting to leave her so soon, but he would not visit her tonight. Not after her fall this afternoon. He may want her every hour of every day, but even he had restraint.

As if reading his mind, she clasped his jaw, pulling him to look at her. "Will you come to me this evening when everyone's abed?" she whispered.

He shook his head, reaching up to wipe away the little frown that appeared between her eyes at his gesture. "You must rest this evening, no matter how much I wish I were not so gallant."

She pouted in disappointment, and he laughed, kissing her before they came too close to the dock. "You are utterly adorable. Where have you been all my life?" he asked her in all seriousness.

"In Cornwall. Do you know," she added, a mischievous light in her eye, "the day I found out I was coming to London, I was trying to catch a pig for dinner. The little rascal would not heed to my will, and just before Mama came outdoors to tell me of the letter from your mama, I had fallen over in pig muck. It was fortunate that the many miles between London and Cornwall are so great, or I could have smelled terrible upon meeting you."

Josh laughed, unable to imagine Iris trying to catch a pig for dinner. "Did you not have servants to do such chores?"

She shrugged. "I had little else to do, so chores of such nature were common for me."

He dipped his head to the crevice of her neck, breathing deep. "You smell quite delicious now, my darling." He ran his tongue along the line of her throat before kissing the lobe of her ear, giving it a small, teasing bite.

Iris gasped, pulling him close. "I want you to visit me this evening. Do not deny me."

He groaned, torn between what was right and what he longed to do. "I should not."

She kissed him, her tongue tangling with his, and he was lost. Unable to deny her anything, or himself for that matter, when it came to her.

As promised, he joined her late that evening and did not leave her room until the early hours in the morning light.

$\mathcal{A}$ week later, the ducal London townhouse was filled with family for the wedding. Iris had welcomed her parents several days ago, and only yesterday Alice, Lady Arndel, arrived with her family. Victoria, Lady Melvin, and her new husband, the marquess, were due to arrive today.

Iris sat in the library with Josh, who worked behind the desk with an array of missives and ledgers open. "I shall get everything here in order, and then we shall be able to take some days away once we're married. I can take you to Dunsleigh if you like. I know I said we would not leave London, but if you wished to return to Surrey, I'm more than happy to comply with your wishes.

Iris strolled about the room, picking up numerous books, reading the spine or the first page or two before slipping it back on the shelf. "Do you think your mama will be lonely should we depart for a week or two? I do not want to leave her alone when she has been so good to me. I should think she's quite used to our company."

The duke leaned back in his chair, placing down his quill. The adoration on his features made her stomach flutter. How was it that the man before her loved her? Adored her? A fact she still struggled to comprehend now, a day before their wedding.

"My sisters will all be staying for several weeks. Alice, in particular, said now that she's back in London, she will not be returning to Surrey anytime soon. Mama will be more than happily occupied. Have you seen how many grandchildren are running about? I think my elder sisters, Isolde and Elizabeth, think this house is a drop-off center for their children to play."

Iris laughed, coming over to lean on the side of his desk. She glanced down at the papers, one letter, in particular, catching her attention. "Is that for me?" she asked, pointing to the neat, flowing script with her name addressed on the front. Someone had opened the letter, and yet, she was sure she had not seen it before.

The duke hesitated, glancing at the desk before shaking his head. "No, a misaddressed missive, that is all."

Iris was unsure what possessed her, but something urged her to see for herself if what Josh said was true. She snatched up the letter. Josh reached for it, and she moved about the other side of the desk. "I will just read it to be sure. I do not want you to have any letters delivered by lady admirers. That will never do." She scanned the contents. Her heart stopped at the words spelled out before her.

"What is this?" she demanded, holding the letter aloft, shaking it.

Josh held out his hand in an attempt to appease her. If what the letter said was true, he had little hope in making her calm.

"There is a person. I'm uncertain if it male or female who wishes to force a wedge between us. I did not want you to know about it."

She thought over his words and what they meant. "Were

you there? Did you see my accident? Were you a part of it?" Her eyes pricked with tears, and she moved farther away from him when he reached for her.

How could he do this to her? How had he not told her? "Did you place a bet to race about Hyde Park and beat your time? Is that why Redgrove did what he did?"

The world spun. Josh had lied to her.

*J*osh fought down the urge to cast up his accounts. Iris had turned a terrible shade of gray. Her eyes, glassy, told him she was on the verge of tears. Damn it all to hell. He should have told her. Weeks ago, he should have been honest and told her all that he knew—his involvement in her accident.

But he had not, and because of her reaction now, he feared losing her.

"Iris, please sit and let me explain."

Surprisingly, she did as he asked. Josh returned to his chair, leaning on his desk and fortifying himself to do something he should have a long time ago.

Even before she had come to town, he should have traveled to Cornwall and told her how very sorry he was and that it was his fault that Redgrove had died. Begged for forgiveness regarding the injuries he had generated.

"Tell me what the letter means," she demanded, a threat of steel in her tone.

"You know that I was familiar with Redgrove before your betrothal was announced. He often came out with us, and we drank and entertained in the same social sphere." He forced his hands to stop shaking, clasping them on his desk. "I played a game with him, knowing how very eager he was to be one of us, even though we never excluded anyone from our set."

"What sort of game did you play?" Her large, blue eyes pinned him to his chair, and he felt the weight of his answer as he debated how to tell her.

"I made a bet in Whites that no one could beat my time around Hyde Park in a curricle. I did not think anyone would bother since it was only a hundred pounds."

Iris scoffed, her eyes wide. "A hundred pounds is a lot of money for some. And Dudley, while being a baron, wasn't flush with cash. Any such gentleman would take up such a bet and put themselves in danger and others. Did you think on that before you made your bet?" she spat at him.

Josh cringed, knowing he had not. "I was arrogant and foolish in my youth. Had you met me then you would not have liked me, Iris. I thought a lot of things were a lark, other than my family."

"And what of the family I was hoping to make with Dudley? Did you never think of others or what your foolish pranks could do?"

He told himself she loved him now, not Redgrove. That yes, they were in the middle of their first argument, but that did not mean all feelings could be erased by his mistake. "I did not, and I'm so sorry, Iris. I did not know what I was doing. I could not see past my own amusement."

"What happened? Tell me. I need to know," she demanded.

Josh ground his teeth, thinking back to that day. He cringed. "Word reached me that Redgrove was going to attempt the bet just before fashionable hour at the park. Along with our set, I arrived to see Redgrove already preparing to race the clock. What I had not expected was for him to have you perched beside him, utterly unaware of what he was about to do."

"I soon found out, though, did I not?"

He took a calming breath, rolling his shoulders. "I started over to you, but Redgrove took off before I could stop him.

He lost control of his set and the carriage on the first corner." The recall of the crunching, sickening sounds of horses rolling with a carriage attached. The sight of Iris flying onto the hardened grounds of the park, of Redgrove hitting a tree, would never dissipate from his memory. It would haunt him until the day he died, just as the look of utter devastation that Iris now had upon her visage would too.

"I cannot tell you how sorry I am. I know no words will ever be enough."

She stood, pacing before his desk. She nibbled on a fingernail, the tears falling unheeded down her cheeks. "You killed Redgrove." She turned and faced him. "Had you not made your stupid damn bet, none of this would have happened. He would be alive today. I would not suffer from my injury. I would not limp when the weather turns chilly. I would not be laughed at for the scar that marred my face. How could you?" she yelled, her hands fisted at her sides as if she were halting herself from striking him. "For months, I suffered. Do you know that after the bone in my leg healed, I was given permission to walk, only for it to fracture a second time when I tried? I hide my pain well. I have lived with it long enough to do so, but this... This is a pain I cannot bear." She strode to the window, and he stood, going to her.

She rounded on him, holding up one finger. "Do not touch me, Your Grace. It is not safe for you to do so right at this moment."

Fuck! His mind scrambled how to make this right. How to fix what he could not change. The past had happened. There was no turning back the clock, no matter how much he wished he could.

He would do anything to make her life different from what it was now. To give her back Redgrove if she wanted, everything, but he could not. Not even a duke had that much power.

"I made a mistake, Iris. I did not know what occurred would happen. I did not know Redgrove would take you on his ride about the park."

"So it is his fault now?"

"No," he went on, not wishing to blame anyone.

"You wrote the bet as a little lark against him. You knew he would take it. That he had me beside him, I grant you was an error, but all of this could be laid at your feet. You wrote the bet." She shook her head, unable to fathom what she had been told. "Templedon hinted that there was more to the accident than I knew, but I never guessed his vague statements would lead to this. How do you live with yourself? How could you court me knowing what you had done to me?"

"I love you. That is why I want to marry you, Iris."

"Oh my God." Her face blanched. "The kiss. Everything between us. You bastard," she sobbed, taking a deep breath to calm herself. "You helped me out of guilt. You felt sorry for me, and that's why you've been so accommodating."

"Iris, that is untrue." Panic assailed him, and he felt along with saw her slipping out of his hold, pulling away from him.

"You pitied me and felt guilty over having a hand in my accident and sustained injuries." She shook her head, clearly bewildered. "I cannot marry you. I will not marry a man who only declares to love me because he feels obligated to save me from a spinsterhood that he had a hand in creating." She wiped at the tears streaming down her cheeks. Josh stood at the desk, completely unsure as to what to do. He would not lose her. No matter what she believed.

"I love you. I have never loved anyone the way I love you," he said, going toward her, only to be turned away yet again. "You are everything to me, and tomorrow we will marry, if only because you could now be carrying my child. But you will marry me, and I will earn your forgiveness. I will make amends for my crime against you and Redgrove. God damn it, Iris, know that I never thought that you would be hurt the way you were. I did not know such a foolish lark would kill Redgrove."

"But we were, weren't we?" She shook her head. "Is that all you care about? That I could be carrying your child? I find out today that you had a hand in the accident that killed my betrothed and then that you kissed me out of pity. You may state otherwise, but it is clear to me as the sky outside that what I say is the truth. My mother may be the daughter of an earl, but I have no dowry or connections to the nobility side of my family. I come to this marriage with nothing but a respectable name. Not that it is so respectable any longer since I have acted without consideration or appropriateness while in town. I'm scarred, have a limp that impedes me when the weather turns cold, and I could not be further from a diamond of the first water, what you wanted for a wife. Do not try to fool me into believing that you kissed me out of anything other than pity. You did not. Nor will I marry you tomorrow. I shall be returning home posthaste where I hope to never set eyes on you again."

Josh stormed after her when she made a break for the door, slamming it shut. "You will marry me, Iris. I never kissed you out of charity."

She made a scoffing sound, refusing to look at him. He ground his teeth. "At least wait and see if you're pregnant first before you cry off. I will not allow my son or daughter to be a bastard."

She did look at him then, and he read the hope seeping out of her blue eyes. Damn it. Now she would think he did not want to marry after all, which could not be further from the truth. He merely needed time. Time to win back her love and trust.

"I will wait until my courses are due, and then we shall

see. Until then, I shall ask my mama to rent a house elsewhere in London. I think it is only right that I leave here."

Josh ran a hand through his hair, fear clutching at his gut that he was losing her. It would be harder for him to repair the damage the truth had wrought with her out of the house. But he would. He would win her love and fix this misunderstanding. And he would marry Iris.

The only duchess who would do for him.

CHAPTER 27

They did not rent another property in London. In fact, much to Iris's surprise, their carriage, bundled with an abundance of luggage, much more than she had arrived in London with rolled to a stop before a large, Georgian Hanover Square manor house. The front covered in ivy, the windows sparkling in the afternoon sun.

"Whose house is this?" Iris asked, glancing in question at her mama.

Her mother waited for the coachman to open the carriage door before climbing down. "My mother's. Come, we shall stay here."

Iris followed her, frowning. Her father came up the rear, quiet and sedate, and Iris wondered what they were doing here. She had made inquiries to call but had been turned down via missive each time. The hand of friendship and forgiveness never outstretched, not even to a grandchild the countess had never met.

Her mama had no need to knock, the door swung wide, and a butler stood, proud and resolute at the door. What happened next made Iris gape. The old retainer's mouth lifted into a genuine smile, and he clasped her mama's hand, pulling her into the house.

"Oh, Lady Jane. How very happy we are to see you. Welcome home," he said, taking in Iris and her father, his smile never fading from his features. "The countess is in the parlor upstairs. I shall take you to her."

Iris cleared her throat. "Should you not check first to see if we will be admitted?" she asked, not wanting to put the countess more against them than she already was.

The footman gave her mama a knowing smile and started climbing the stairs leading to the first floor. "How is the countess, John?" her mother queried, her voice without fear, merely genuine curiosity.

Iris could make no sense of the situation at all. They disliked her mama's family. She was sure of it. What was happening here made as much sense as her betrothal to the Duke of Penworth.

Very little, and ended just as bad as her mother's relationship with the countess they were about to meet.

"She will be all the better for seeing you, Lady Jane," the butler stated.

They reached the first floor and turned down a long passage that opened up to a bank of windows, numerous family paintings down one side. Iris halted at the sight of her mama, a painting of her during her coming-out season. She gasped and felt her father halt, his attention too caught on the magnificent artwork.

"How beautiful mama was," Iris declared, noting the family diamonds that adorned her mother's neck and hair.

"Your mama is still as beautiful as that woman in the painting to me. I should have made her go see her mother and make amends years ago. It was my own fault that they fell out."

They continued on. Iris riveted to the story she had never

heard before, but one her father seemed willing to share. "What happened, Papa?" she asked, having wanted to know for some years now.

He pursed his lips. "The short of it was she married a man who was the third son of a baron when she should have married a duke such as yourself."

Iris did not correct her father that she was yet to marry the duke, and right at this moment, was unlikely to do so. Not after what he had done to her. The lies and hurt he had caused her.

As if on cue, her leg protested her step, and she flinched.

Her father continued, "We married against her parents' wishes, and she was cut off without a penny to her name. They told her never to return unless she had come to her senses."

Iris frowned, wondering what it meant that they were here now then. Her father must have read her mind, for he chuckled. "I'm sure she's not about to throw me over now, but I do think your mama's about to wrap her mother about her finger again and by using you to gain her forgiveness. The countess, no matter how harsh she was to me, loved her daughter, and I do think it broke her heart that they have not mended their relationship in all these years."

"I'm sorry to put you and Mama in this situation. I know the wedding was supposed to proceed tomorrow, but I'm not ready. Not yet. I need time, you understand, do you not, Papa?" she begged him, knowing that her father would always stand beside her and her decisions.

"Of course, my darling. We would never force you into a union you were not ready for."

They came to the drawing room, and if Iris thought to see dull, gray furnishings and black curtains, blocking out the light, hiding the immovable and cruel countess from the world beyond, she was utterly mistaken.

Bright-yellow silk wallpaper covered the walls. Soft greens and pastel shades of every color you could imagine covered the furnishings and rugs upon the floors.

She watched from the doorway as the countess stood at their arrival, her eyes alight with shock and hope. Her mother, the countess's only daughter, dipped into a perfect curtsy, throwing her mama a knowing smile. "My lady, Mother," she said, continuing to grin in a way that Iris recognized as a secret little look between mother and daughter.

"Jane?" the countess said, her voice wobbling with emotion. "You are here?"

She nodded. "I thought it time we were friends again. Too much time has passed, and as you know, I have had a happy and loving marriage to a good man who is now a vicar. And I need your support now, more than ever, if we're to help Iris keep her reputation if she cries off permanently her wedding to Penworth."

The older woman's gray hair was still curled and pinned to perfection on her head. Her skin was wrinkled with time, but Iris could still see the resemblance of a young, beautiful woman, a daughter of a marquess if she were not mistaken, staring over to her.

"So you are the woman everyone is talking about this Season. The very lady who captured the elusive duke's heart. Come, my granddaughter, and let me have a look at you."

Iris came before the countess, dipping into a curtsy, still unable to believe that any of them were here.

"I'm sorry I have not allowed you to call, you must forgive my past judgements on others and let us move forward."

Iris cast a curious glance to her mama, who rolled her eyes at the countess's words.

"Now, let me look at you, dear." Iris waited for the countess to complete her inspection. "Hmm, yes, you do look pale and in need of rest. I'll have your rooms prepared." The countess patted Iris's cheek. "It is lovely to meet you, at last. I'm happy your mama came to her senses and decided to bring you here to meet me. I shall do all that I can to ensure your Season is still a success even if the duke is no longer part of your life."

The weight of the situation became all too much and Iris sought out a settee to sit without being invited to do so. She slumped into the chair, the grandmother she just met and her mama coming to sit on either side of her. "I do not know what I want any longer," she admitted truthfully. "Or what I should do."

Her father bowed, backing out of the room. "I shall allow you ladies to discuss the matters of the heart alone. I will be in the library downstairs should you need me."

Iris looked after her father, who all but ran from the room. A lump wedged in her throat over her argument with Josh only hours ago. The hasty packing. The tears, both hers and the dowager duchess's, who had no idea that her son had any part in Redgrove's misfortune. What a terrible day it had been for everyone.

"Tell me what has happened, my dear. I'm the Countess Buttersworth, and I shall make it all better. I promise you that. and if not, I shall send you on a grand trip abroad with myself as your chaperone, and we shall enjoy the sights the continent has to offer."

"Mama, do be serious," Lady Jane chastised. "Iris is yet to understand your teasing. She's upset, can you not see? You need to be serious."

"Bah," the countess barked. "I have been serious for years, and it left me without a daughter. I will no longer be so." The countess reached across Iris and clasped her daughter's hand. "I'm so very glad you have come home, my dear. Even if you did bring your husband whom I shall accept, but always believe far beneath your notice. Even so," she continued, "I'm glad that you are back under this roof."

Iris's mama squeezed the countess's hands in return. "I am glad to be here too. I should have come many years ago. But, I suppose I get my stubbornness from my mother and refused to bend."

The countess chuckled then sobered. "Now, tell me what occurred that this engagement seems to be halted all of a sudden. I will not mention that I did not receive an invitation to the nuptials."

Iris felt the heat on her cheeks. Her mother shrugged. "I was mad at you, that is why you did not receive an invite, but that is all forgotten now, isn't it, Mama? Now we must concentrate on the next generation of our family."

"Oh, of course. Of course. Iris dear, do fill me in what was said between you and the duke."

Like a tidal wave of words, she blurted out what happened between them. The kiss that brought upon their engagement in the first place. The many hints and vague statements from Templedon and Lady Sophie. She excluded the information about the duke and herself being intimate. They did not need to know all her secrets. But then she told them the worst part, by far. That the duke had made the bet that Redgrove had taken upon himself to best and the outcome that they all knew occurred. She told them that he had only helped her out of pity because he felt guilty over his involvement in her accident.

She fumbled in her reticule for her handkerchief, dabbing at her nose and cheeks. "I cannot marry the duke, and you can see why not. He does not love me. He feels sorry for me. Sees me as some cripple that requires saving and he, the brave knight in shining armor."

"He is certainly handsome enough to be a knight," her

grandmother quipped. "Tell us what the duke replied to your accusations."

Iris sniffed, hating to remember. "That is was untrue." That he kissed her because he wanted to. That she had been in his thoughts for days leading up to their slip of etiquette. "That he did not feel sorry for me and did not propose because his mother caught us and made him."

"Did the dowager make him propose?" her mother queried.

Iris thought back on the day. "No, she did not. The duke beat her to it and stated he was merely kissing in celebration of his new fiancée." The memory did take a little sting out of the situation but were his words this afternoon true? Or was he lying yet again, evading the truth as he had done so for weeks about his bet that killed Redgrove?

"I think," her mama said, "that you should take some time to think over everything that has happened. There is no shame in waiting. You have had a shock with what you were told. I'm certain that it has brought up painful memories from your past and made you question the duke's motives. Anyone having been told what you were would feel the same."

Her mama's words comforted her. What the duke had spoken had upset her. Had made her question his loyalty, his love for her. How could it not? Their union was not expected. Not even she had thought to marry so far above her station. That he had possibly proposed because he felt responsible, guilty over her injuries was a truth she could not stomach. No marriage would survive or be a happy union with such an unstable foundation.

"I'm very tired. Would you mind if I excused myself and rested in my room?"

"Of course, my dear. I should want to catch up with your mama in any case." The butler, as if sensing the countess was about to summon him, came into the room. "Please escort my granddaughter to the guest suite, John."

He bowed and did as he was bid. Iris followed the gentleman, exhaustion overtaking her limbs and making them weak. In a week or so, she would know if she would have to marry the duke. While a part of her longed for a child, his child to be precise, she also did not want to be forced into a union that she did not long for.

Had his guilt over his involvement in Redgrove's downfall clouded his judgment when it came to her? Made him believe he had to be her savior, her protector?

The butler halted at a door not far along the passage. "This is the guest suite, Miss Cooper. Please let us know if you require anything. I'll have a lady's maid sent up to assist you shortly."

"Thank you," she replied, going into the room and sitting on the edge of the bed. The room was feminine and light, the windows overlooking Hanover Square. Carriages rolled by, and families took the air in the park across the road. A tear rolled down her cheek, and she swiped at it. How could her life, her union with the duke have gone so terribly wrong?

But she did know how it had come to pass, and now she needed to figure out what to do about it. If anything was to be done about it at all.

CHAPTER 28

A week after Iris had left his London home, Josh sat in the library, penning yet another letter to her, begging for her to forgive him. To come home and marry him.

He knew she would not. With the days passing by and not a word from her, a sinking, irreparable feeling had settled in his gut and would not dissipate. London and their postponed wedding was all the *ton* were talking about. The chatter, the sly looks, and amused glances that some of the women threw his way, was unbearable.

They all ought to be horsewhipped. Hell, he ought to be belted too for what he had done and not said to Iris. A shameful secret such as the one he kept from her was never appropriate.

It would serve him right if she should leave him and never return. Marry someone else much nobler than he. A gentleman who had not stripped her of her betrothed and then hidden that fact from her while courting her to marry.

Hell, he'd not even done that. He'd kissed her and had merely announced their betrothal. He had not asked her for her hand or queried whether she was willing to have him as her husband. Therefore, it did not surprise him that Iris did not believe a word he spoke about his feelings being genuine.

Now she would not allow him to call, every missive he had sent returned unopened. He doubted she would ever do so again. He had buggered up everything and was at a loss over how to repair the damage.

How could he win back her love? He threw down his quill, the ink splattering upon his mahogany desk, and leaned back in his chair.

The sound of the library door closing had him looking up. For a moment, hope bloomed through his chest that Iris had come to call on him, to discuss their future, but instead, his sister Alice stood in the doorway, her eyes clouded with concern.

She came over to the desk, seating herself across from him. "What have you done, Josh darling? I know it is bad, for I just ran into Iris on Bond Street, she was out with the countess, and she barely spoke a word to me. She was very subdued. Whatever has occurred between you two that she is now pulling away from us all?"

"Iris was on Bond Street?" The urge to ride down there and see if she was still present ate at him. Josh forced himself not to move. She would come to him when she was ready to talk. He would not force her, not when his life and happiness depended on her choosing him.

"She was, and although she was friendly and polite, I had a distinct feeling that she was also wary. Why are you both not already married? Mama has been vague as to the reason why you are not. I need to know so I can fix this."

Josh ran a hand through his hair. His sister Alice—always the woman determined to make other people's lives better. Her housing in Ashford for the poor proof of that. Her inability to allow justice to go unserved by those who deserved to be chastised legendary in the family. Her husband was alive today because she refused to let anything bad happen to him when others threatened him harm.

"This, dear sister, I think even you may not be able to repair. I have broken trust with Iris. I have lied to her, and she will not forgive me for it."

Alice blanched. "Tell me, brother you did not sleep with a whore at Covent Gardens or some other such locale. I will not forgive you if you have done such a cruel act."

Josh scowled. "Of course I have not. I would never treat her with so little respect." But he had, of course, treated her wrong. Had lied to her with a truth that was so much worse than a mistress could impact on her heart. "I posted the bet in the Whites betting book that her betrothed took upon himself to participate in. Redgrove was his name, and he chose Iris to accompany him on his race about Hyde Park. As you are well aware, he was killed, and Iris was maimed. I kept that truth from her of my involvement in his race, and when she found out, as hurt and as angry as she was over my conduct, she now believes I only proposed out of guilt."

Alice's eyes went wide, and for a breath or two, she did not speak. "Did you ask her to marry you because you felt blameworthy?"

"Of course not," he stated truthfully. "But how do I make Iris believe that? She will not, I fear. She is angry at me for creating the bet in the first place, but when she concluded that our engagement was a farce..." He paused, running a hand through his hair. "Her face, Alice. If devastation had a look, she wore it, and never have I wanted to kick my own ass so much in my life."

"Darling brother, you are not a bad man. You made a mistake, and so too did Redgrove. While you should not have made such a bet, Redgrove should not have had Miss Cooper with him that day." Alice stood and went over to the decanter of whisky, pouring him a glass, placing it down before him. "Your other predicament that Iris thinks you proposed out of guilt is another issue altogether, and I fear a much weightier problem."

Did he not know it. "Do you not think I understand that?" he snapped, downing his drink, the burn of the amber liquid a welcome pain for his already distressed body.

"You must make amends, and I fear it will need to be a grand gesture of some sort." She sat back down, chewing her nails in thought. "As to what, however, we shall need to think and plan."

Josh studied his sister, wondering not for the first time if she had gone a little mad. Alice was untamed and wild at heart. It would not surprise him if she, too, were a little deranged. A grand gesture indeed. He could never do such a thing. He was the Duke of Penworth. Gentlemen looked up to him. They would never do so again if he acted the lovesick fool trying to win back his betrothed.

You are a lovesick fool trying to win back your betrothed.

"I will not be partaking in a grand gesture."

"No?" Alice queried. "So you're willing to lose her, let her marry another? I do not think so," she said, wagging her finger at him. "Why has the wedding been postponed but not called off? I'm curious what the delay of that decision meant."

Heat rose on his cheeks, and his sister raised her brows. "Brother, tell me you have not taken liberties that you should not have. Is Iris *enceinte?*"'

He groaned, downing his drink. "We do not know. She said her courses were due this week. I have not heard the outcome of this as yet." He glanced at his sister. "And you are one to criticize me over my dealings with Iris. You were not an angel when Lord Arndel moved in next door to Dunsleigh."

She shrugged, throwing him a bored look. "It is lucky

then, is it not, that I'm now Lady Arndel and no harm was done. If you have compromised Iris, and she does throw you to the curb and marries another, what will happen if her husband finds out she has given you liberties you did not deserve? If he decides to punish her for her past, she will be ousted from society and sent packing to live in the country. It would be best if you fixed everything that you have wrought on the girl, and soon. Before it is too late."

He lifted the many letters written and returned. "I have been trying. She will not hear a word about anything."

"Then you must make her listen. She is yours, brother. You must make her remember the truth. That you have made a mistake but want to make amends. That you want her for who she is, not what you have done to her." Alice stood, placing her hands on her hips. "Now get off your chair and onto a horse and go win back my future sister-in-law. We have a wedding to hold."

Determination shot through his blood at his sister's words. "You are right. I shall demand to see her, make her believe me."

"Very good," his sister said, gesturing for the door. "No time like the present."

No time indeed.

Josh called at the Countess Buttersworth's London home within an hour of his conversation with Alice, only to be told the ladies were not at home and that they were not expected to return for several hours. Josh waited across the street, parked under a large oak tree, but the family did not return as stated by the butler.

They were due to attend the Davies ball this evening. An event no one dared miss, not even his family, and he hoped as he rapped his cane on the roof of the carriage to return home that Iris too would be there.

He wanted to see her. That he had not held her in his

arms for seven days was more than he could bear. He loved her. She needed to believe that if nothing else.

*I*ris sat in the carriage on the way to the Davies ball, her stomach churning, but not from the fear of seeing Josh, but the agonizing realization that her courses were not far away now and would begin within a day or two.

The cramping and bloating she gained just before her monthly bleeding was always the same, and there was no reason why her body would react any different now, even though she was no longer a maid.

She would be safe enough tonight, but from tomorrow she would remain close to home. It was safer that way, for her courses had always been less than pleasant.

She would have to tell Josh, of course, that she was not carrying his child. The truth would free her from any obligation to marry him. He could do as he wished from tonight onward. Please himself without concern.

She inwardly cursed her bruised, angry heart and hurtful thoughts upon a man who would never treat her with such disrespect.

But he had treated you so, you silly fool.

The carriage rolled to a halt, and her mama and grandmother paid their respects to the hostesses before they entered the ballroom. Iris counted the chandeliers that ran down the center of the room, eight in total. Gold leaf glittered on every surface and paintings that hung about the room. The silk floral wallpaper made the room one of richness and abundance.

The guests they passed tittered and whispered, and Iris raised her chin, refusing to cower at their gossip. She had done nothing wrong. Not really. As far as they were aware, the wedding was still going ahead, merely delayed at this stage. She may have relocated to her grandmother's home, but there was nothing wrong with that.

She stood with her family, looking about and hoping there would be a chair nearby, but there was not. In fact, the ball did not look to have any available in the room at all.

Iris steeled herself for an evening that would result in her leg aching for days afterward.

"The duke is here, my dear," her mama whispered.

Iris's attention snapped to the ballroom doors, her heart doing a little flip in her chest at the sight of Josh. How utterly, devastatingly handsome he was this evening in his superfine coat and silk knee-high breeches.

He was perfection, and she physically hurt at the thought of losing him, of him marrying another in the years or months ahead stopped her heart dead. But that was for the best. She was not pregnant, and she would not be anyone's pity wife. He said that he loved her, but did he? Or was that too just a means to make himself feel better?

He certainly had kept the knowledge of his dealings with Redgrove a secret, so she knew him to be capable of anything to save himself from confrontation. It was only left to be seen what he would say and do tonight to save himself with her.

Or end their union forever.

CHAPTER 29

*L*ady Sophie intercepted the duke as he made his way toward Miss Cooper. It was all that London spoke. That Lady Jane was back from Cornwall, back within the folds of her wealthy family and bringing her daughter Miss Cooper into the realm of that world with her.

Although Sophie was not privy to how Lady Jane was able to gain forgiveness for marrying the dreadful younger son of a penniless baron, it seemed all was forgiven if their little party of three, which included the Countess Buttersworth, was anything to go by.

Sophie smiled as she brought the duke to a halt. He crashed into her, a perfect end to her accosting him and would make him clasp her, worry about her health for a minute or two, which was all she needed.

She gasped, clasping her chest, and as expected, the duke held her elbow, just beside where her silk glove ended. His warm, gloved hand touched her skin, and she shivered at the feel of him.

How she wished he would be hers, and after tonight, she was determined that it would be so.

"I do apologize, Lady Sophie. I did not see you there," he said, letting her go when he was certain she was well and stable.

Sophie stumbled, moaning a little. He took her arm once again. "Oh dear, perhaps I have had a little wind knocked out of me, Your Grace. Will you escort me onto the terrace for some air?"

He hesitated, glancing past her, no doubt toward his intended, and she waved his hesitation aside. "I shall go, and I will be fine. You carry on to where you were heading." Sophie turned to go out onto the terrace herself and inwardly smiled when the duke came up beside her, placing her hand atop his arm.

"Forgive me, Lady Sophie. That was uncommonly rude of me, especially when I was the fool who knocked into you in the first place. Of course, I shall escort you outside for some air."

They made their way through the room, and Sophie could not help but glance over her shoulder. The sight of Miss Cooper, watching them, a dejected, worried kind of frown upon her pathetic features, just what Sophie wanted to see. She turned back to the duke and mentioned the warm night air as they stepped out onto the flagstone terrace.

Other parties of acquaintances stood outdoors, talking and smoking their cheroots. Couples strolled, and Sophie glanced up at the night sky, thanking the heavens that she finally had the duke alone. Well, away from Miss Cooper in any case.

"Thank you for escorting me. I already feel much improved."

He smiled and kept them within view of the other guests taking the air. "Of course." He cleared his throat. "How are you enjoying the Season, my lady? I do hope it's been as productive as I would expect it to be."

She threw him a coy glance, watching him from under her lashes. "Do you say that because you think I'm attractive, Your Grace?" she boldly stated.

His mouth opened, his lips moved, but no sound came out.

Sophie chuckled. "I am teasing, Your Grace. But the season has been less stellar than I hoped. But I'm here now, strolling with you, so it is improving by the hour." Sophie held his gaze, wanting him to see that she hoped their association would progress further than mere acquaintances. She wanted him as her husband. They were made for each other —equal levels on the social ladder.

He smiled, but she could feel the tension in his arms. "It is most enjoyable outdoors this evening, I would agree, and it is always pleasant to walk with friends."

Sophie bit back a groan. The man was playing hard to get, but she would persist. "There is a rumor that your engagement to Miss Cooper is at an end." She pulled him to a stop, taking his hand. "I do hope you know that as your friend, I'm very sorry for you if that is the case. If there is anything I can do to soften the blow to your heart, I'm more than willing to oblige you."

Josh stood rooted to the spot, unable to form a word of response to Lady Sophie and her blatant admission of interest. Never had a woman so highly born who was not already a widow disclosed such a suggestion before.

Had he never met Iris, Lady Sophie's attempt to persuade him into a liaison, a union, would never have occurred. While she would pass as a friendly acquaintance and he never bore her ill will, he did not see her in the romantic sense.

Nor was his engagement with Iris at an end, and it would never be if he could fix their relationship. His being out here on the terrace with Lady Sophie was not helpful either.

"My betrothal to Miss Cooper is not at an end, and I should hope you will dissuade people of that opinion should you hear the rumor repeated. In fact, before I so rudely ran into you, I was starting toward my betrothed and really ought to return to her." He held out his hand. "Let me escort you back indoors."

He read the disappointment on her face, the tightening of her mouth, but she laid her gloved hand atop his and conceded defeat. "Oh dear, I do hope Miss Cooper is not under the belief that we're now courting. How dreadful of me to have made your relationship with her more challenging."

"Miss Cooper would not think that way," he quipped, hoping he was right. As they made their way along the terrace, three ladies stepped outside, Iris's accusing blue gaze pinning him to the spot.

That Lady Sophie sidled up closer to him, leaning into him as if they were lovers, did not help the situation. Josh tried to remove himself from Lady Sophie's clutches without making a scene, but it was impossible. She was wedged firmly at his side.

"Your Grace," the countess spat his name like it was wicked on her tongue, her cane tapping down hard once before her. "Are you so busy escorting other young ladies about town that you have forgotten to whom you are engaged?"

Josh swore. He had never wanted to come out here in the first place, but having almost barrelled Lady Sophie over, it was the least he could do as a gentleman. "I was coming to find you, Miss Cooper. I wanted to ask if you would like to dance."

Iris stared at him, her gaze flicking between himself and Lady Sophie. The accusation in her eyes chilled him. She was already angry with him over his keeping such a devastating secret from her that this only added fuel to the firestorm burning between them.

He swallowed, extricating himself from Lady Sophie less gracefully than he would like. "Come, Iris. We shall dance."

She cast a look at her mother and grandmother, but to his surprise, conceded, choosing not to make any more of a scene. Not that she had made any. Lady Sophie was doing a fine job of that all on her own.

"Lady Sophie, let us go inside for a glass of Madeira," he heard Lady Jane state, her voice brooking no argument.

Josh led Iris onto the ballroom floor. The feel of her in his arms, her warmth and sweet scent that he had come to associate wholly with Iris, warmed his blood. He'd missed her this past week, and it was past time that they spoke.

He pulled her into the waltz, glad to have her all to himself. "I have missed you," he stated, trying to catch her eye, which she was steadfastly avoiding. "Why have you not allowed me to call or received my letters?"

Her lips thinned, and he steeled himself. Was she angrier than he suspected? Mayhap she was unable to forgive him his sins. Was he pushing her too hard too soon after learning the truth?

"I was not ready to speak to you or read anything from you. I'm allowed to be angry for more than a day over your conduct, Your Grace."

"I thought we were on first-name terms. Please, do not start calling me Your Grace again. I'm Josh to you."

She took a calming breath, finally meeting his gaze. "I am not pregnant. There is no reason why our farce of an engagement should continue. I would like the contracts dissolved and soon so I may return to Cornwall with my parents."

Josh tripped during the dance, righting himself quickly. "What? You cannot mean what you say. We have not discussed the situation as much as we should. You have not had time to think clearly on the matter, to find forgiveness for my sins."

"And why should I forgive such sin? You lied to me. There is nothing to say that you will not do so again should the situation arise and you find it easier to be vague and untruthful to save yourself. I will not be a wife to you when it is clearly only an offer because we were caught. You kissed me, and I believe you kissed me out of pity and guilt. Nothing will dissuade me of that."

The hell nothing would dissuade her of those thoughts. "You will marry me, Iris. I will not listen to these absurd words that I know you do not mean."

"But I do mean them. I cannot see a way forward for us. Not with everything that stands between us." She caught his gaze, the shimmer of tears in her blue orbs breaking his heart in two. "I do not trust you, and I will not have my husband pity me, marry me out of that emotion. I suffer from such treatment from others, I could not bear it from the man I marry. No matter how difficult our separation may be, I know that it is what is best."

He went to protest, but she shook her head, stopping him. "I am not what you want, Your Grace. I never was. Seeing you tonight on the terrace with Lady Sophie... That is the kind of woman you ought to marry. Not me. We never fit, and there is a reason women like me do not marry duke's like you."

Josh could feel her pulling away. He could not lose her. "Do not do this, Iris. If I could take back time and tell you everything from the start, I would, but I cannot. We suit, more than I befit anyone else. I love you. Please do not leave me."

She looked past him, cold and aloof. "You will find a woman who meets your high expectations, and you will be relieved, maybe not at first, but in time that you did not settle for a vicar's daughter. Your wife will be beautiful, capable, and not scarred, just as you stipulated."

"I was a selfish, immature idiot when I said those things. I did not mean them."

She shrugged. "Let me go, Josh. I'm begging you not to make a scene or make this any more difficult than it already is."

Panic assailed him. What was happening here? The room spun, and he fought to breathe. She was leaving him. Truly? It was not possible that she would not see reason. Not want to fight for the love he knew they shared, even if she no longer believed in that emotion between them.

"I will not let you walk away from me when I know that we're meant to be together. You walked into my life, came into my world for a reason. That reason is love. Please, let me earn your trust. Let me prove to you that my love is true."

The music receded to a stop, and he swooped her to a halt. They stood in the middle of the room, other couples moving about them, preparing for the next dance. "There is nothing that you can do that will change my mind. Good evening, Your Grace," she stated, dipping into a curtsy.

Dumbfounded, he watched her walk away, spine straight and chin high, toward her family. Neither the countess nor Lady Jane offered any sign that they had seen him. They simply followed Iris out of the ballroom and out of sight.

"Fuck it," he muttered, leaving those about him wide-eyed and pale at his words. He departed also, determined to repair the damage, to fix what he had so obviously broken.

Their relationship was not over, nor would it ever be.

CHAPTER 30

*I*ris did not know what to do. The memory of Josh's crushed visage at the Davies ball the evening before made her stomach drop to the floor. She had been cold and aloof, uncaring and curter than she had ever been with anyone in her life.

He deserved her wrath, she knew. To be told such a hurtful truth was not something that a person could simply get over in a day. It would take her time to digest what she now knew of her betrothed. His actions during her first Season and the outcome of those actions. But more hurtful than anything had been the horrible thought that he wanted her only out of compassion. Another way to soothe his troubled conscience.

She would not have it. She would not marry anyone under those circumstances.

Her mother and grandmother were in the upstairs parlor, an abundance of sewing around them. Her father had relocated to the library, and Iris sat in the morning room alone, looking out onto her grandmother's London home gardens.

Whatever would she do? Last evening she had told the duke that their union was at an end, but was it?

Could she find forgiveness for him if given the time to understand, if she ever could understand such an untruth? The actions he had made, the outcome they had caused.

But he was so very sorry, and no one who made a bet ever wished for anyone to be injured by it. The duke would not have expected Redgrove to die during the farce that day.

The matter relating to herself was more troublesome. He had been so adamant that his wife would be a diamond of the first water, perfect in every way, that to offer to her could not be borne out of genuine feelings.

It simply could not be. His guilt had to have been a factor. She was certain of it.

But could she trust him again? Forgive him that sin also?

Iris frowned down at the cup of tea in her hand, uncertain she could.

A knock sounded on the door, startling her before the butler announced Lady Arndel was here, wanting to know if she were at home.

Iris accepted her visit, and within a minute, Josh's sister strode into the room, her long, dark locks bouncing about her shoulders. Iris had heard the woman was a little hoyden before she married, and she could believe that very well from the mischief that seemed to ooze off her in spades.

"Miss Cooper," Lady Arndel said, bussing her cheeks in welcome as if they were already sisters-in-law. Iris would have liked to have been a part of Josh's family, to gain Josh's sisters as her own extended family was a boon to an only child.

She supposed if she were to leave town, bring to an end to their understanding, she would no longer have such a gift. Another blow and too many that she had suffered this week.

"How lovely to see you again. We have missed you at

home, and I thought I would call on you today and see how well you are faring."

She was not faring well. Life had lost a little of its luster, a little of its shine, and at this time, she could not see it ever coming back again. Still, she lied. "I am well, thank you. I would have called, but under the circumstances, I did not think it was best." Iris gestured to the settee. "Please sit. I have fresh tea if you would like a cup."

Lady Arndel poured her own before Iris had a chance to do so then settled back in her chair. "That is what I wanted to discuss with you. My call is not merely for entertainment value. I have been charged to speak with you and see what you plan to do."

Iris wondered how much Josh had told his family, not only about their troubles but the reason behind them. "I assumed His Grace had explained his dealings with Redgrove."

Alice sipped her tea but nodded. "We have discussed it, and I understand that it is something very difficult to understand and take in. I know I would not accept such truth if I were in your position, but I'm also the sister of the man who loves you, and I could not come here today without trying one last time to change your mind."

The situation was not ideal. She had gone over what she could remember of the day of her accident, which was very little. But one thing she had been debating and dissecting, again and again, was that Dudley had chosen to take her in the carriage with him. In all her anger at the duke, the distrust that rose its ugly head at hearing the fact, she had not mulled over Dudley's involvement in her accident.

Why had he chosen to take her on the race around Hyde Park? Why had the silly man attempted the stupid bet during a busy time at the park where children, families, and couples strolled and took in the air?

"I have not been without conflict, Lady Arndel. This past week has been the worst of my life, and I did not think anything would be worse than waking up with a fractured leg, a scarred, stitched temple, and a dead fiancé, but here I am. My heart was not broken this time; it was shattered."

"The duke would take back the day he wrote that bet in the book at Whites if he could, but he cannot. I'm hoping you will find it in your heart to forgive him. He is miserable without you, Miss Cooper. Your fear that he asked for your hand out of guilt and not love is not founded. I know my little brother, and I have never seen him so gutted over anything in his life. And I have known him all of mine."

Iris swiped at a tear that rolled down her cheek. She fumbled for her handkerchief. "I have come to understand that it was not the duke's fault for my accident. Yes, he did place the bet in Whites, and although I suppose a small allocation of blame will always weigh on his shoulders, my late betrothed Redgrove chose to attempt the bet, and with me along with him." Iris sighed, tired of it all. Tired of her injuries, of her anxiety over what people thought of her and her scars. Tired of not believing that even with all that came up against her, tried to tear her down and maim her both physically and mentally, that she was not worthy of love.

She was worthy of love, and she needed to believe Josh when he told her he loved her. Not out of guilt, but because he loves every part of her. Of who and what she is.

Lady Arndel reached out and patted her hand. "No matter how it came about that you were sponsored by my mama. No matter how you came to be thrown into the same orbit as my brother, know this, for it is true. He has fallen in love with you, Miss Cooper. Nothing in your past or his matters if you love him in return."

Lady Arndel sat back, placing down her teacup and busying herself, pouring another cup. "My husband was married before me and had a child, a daughter before I married him. He was also in a lot of strife due to the cousin he inherited the title from being in debt. My husband stole from me, was the Surrey Bandit, not that you heard that from me, you understand." Lady Alice pinned her with a look that declared she was never to speak of it again. "I saved him, of course, from himself, and those who threatened him and our new family together. You see, Iris, if you will allow me to call you that."

Iris nodded, riveted and not willing to disavow her.

"He held my carriage up at gunpoint, stole jewels, and accosted me, but his honesty, his determination to make amends soothed my injured heart, and I found myself in love with the man before I even knew it was happening. If I can find forgiveness and have the happiest life one could imagine with a man, I know to the very core of my soul that you can too. That if you choose to forgive, you will find peace and love, and passion and every good thing that you deserve."

Iris could not hold back the tears, and she dabbed at her cheeks, willing her heart to calm, her stomach to settle over Lady Arndel's words. "I had no idea that the Surrey Bandit attacked you. I do remember reading of him. I never imagined..."

"That is was Callum?" Lady Arndel chuckled. "I was attracted to the fellow, even as he accosted me. It led me to wonder who he was, and his horse was magnificent. I was not overly surprised when I found out it was our titled neighbor, and then I had to make him pay."

Iris was quite captivated with the story and would ask about it further at another time. "I'm to attend Robinson's masked ball this evening. Do you know if Josh will be there? I did receive a missive this morning from your mama, and it stated that His Grace was traveling outside of London today to attend business."

"Yes, he's looking at purchasing some land, I believe. He thinks it will be a good investment or some such," Alice said with a disinterested wave. "I know he will be in attendance this evening, for he hopes to see you. You are traveling back to Cornwall tomorrow."

"Yes, that is what is planned." But Iris was no longer so certain of her decision. She would always mourn Dudley, but he had chosen to attempt the bet and have her along with him for the ride. A silly mistake he could never take back. Josh, too, had played a part, but it was cruel of her to blame him entirely. It was not his fault.

Iris thought over Alice's words that the duke adored and loved her, not out of guilt but because he loved her for who and what she was. Could she believe that? Could she trust that his affection was from an emotional and physical attraction and not because of what she had gone through, what had become of her due to the bet?

"I will speak with His Grace this evening. I will discuss our future with him. While I do not know what I shall do, I promise I shall give him one last opportunity to say what he must."

Alice smiled, placing down her tea and coming over to her. Iris stood and found herself in a tight embrace. "You are worthy of love, Miss Cooper, as we all are. He loves you, and you will see this evening how much my proud, duke of a brother does. I shall see you this evening." Lady Arndel kissed Iris's cheeks and then flounced out of the room, as quickly and as determinedly as she had stepped into it.

Iris slumped down onto the settee, thinking of Lady Arndel's last words. What did they mean? If anything at all. Her mind cleared a little for the first time in a week before she stood and started for her room. She wanted to look her best this evening, her last in London or perhaps if fate had a different plan for her, the start of many more.

CHAPTER 31

The second masquerade ball was a crush. The room swam with color, with gowns of gold and greens, silks and tulle. Masks covered most attendee's faces. The laughter and chatter were deafening. Iris moved through the room with her mama and grandmother, who also sported dominoes and matching masks.

The two women had grown close within the week they had spent together, and Iris knew no matter what happened with her and the duke, her mother and grandmother would spend a lot more time together in the coming years. The rift in the family finally healed.

The orchestra in Lord and Lady Robinson's home was situated on an upstairs mezzanine floor, overlooking the ballroom itself. Iris stood across from it near the bank of windows that overlooked the grounds of the London townhouse. The gardens beyond were illuminated with torches, people too outside on the terrace and lawns enjoying the night of revelry.

A footman came up to them and forgoing the ratafia, Iris

picked up a glass of wine, feeling the need for fortification to do what she must this evening.

After Lady Arndel had left, she had spent the day thinking about her life. What she wanted and longed for most. What she was able to forgive and forget, and she knew that she could forgive Josh.

But only if he were truly in love with her and she was not some charity old maid he felt sorry for.

If he declared himself with that truth, then she too would believe him at his word. She would trust that he stated the truth and believe in his love.

Iris laughed as her father joined them, and scooped her mama out on the dance floor, her mother's squeal of delight bringing a smile to her grandmother's face.

"Oh, how I shall miss you all when you leave. I think it is time that I visited Cornwall and see where my grand-daughter grew up." The countess cupped Iris's cheeks in her hands. "I should have forgiven your mama her choice and let go of the pain and disappointment her marriage brought against me a long time ago, Iris dear. I'm sorry I hurt you all," the countess said before she too was pulled away in conversation by other acquaintances.

Forgiveness.

There was that word again. Mumbled to her for what felt like the hundredth time in under a day. Was it a sign from the heavens that she too ought to let go, step forward into a new life, a new time and forget the past?

The orchestra's tune faded out, and Iris looked up to see why they would stop playing in the middle of a waltz and gaped at the sight of Josh. He was unmasked and without a domino—no hiding himself from the *ton* below.

She cast a glance about the room. Everyone's attention was riveted on him and what he was doing up there. This was one of the most sought-after balls in the Season, the last masquerade held this year. Everyone who was anyone in town was present.

An eager whisper, questions murmured through the crowd, before Josh, who was studying everyone beneath him, locked eyes with her.

Oh, dear.

Iris's stomach fluttered at the sight of him, handsome and broad-shouldered. A powerful duke demanding an audience.

But why? What would he say to them all?

When the duke had the room's full attention, no hairpin dared drop to the parquetry floor. Only then did he start to speak.

His deep, rich baritone wrapped about her like a soothing balm. How she had missed his voice. His presence. His everything.

"Good evening, ladies and gentlemen. I have come here this evening, for one reason and one reason only. And, fortunate for those of you present here this evening, you are about to find out why."

Again, whispers ran the length of the room, but Iris could not look away. She felt a hand slip around hers and welcomed the comfort of her grandmother at her side.

"This Season, you have been aware that my mother, the Dowager Duchess Penworth sponsored Miss Iris Cooper. Her first Season was cut short due to an accident, and I'm here today to pay penance for my involvement on that terrible day and to seek forgiveness. I also stand before you because there are truths that need acknowledging without another day passing."

Iris heard the blood pumping in her ears, and for a moment, she wondered if she would faint. She steeled herself to listen, to hear him out his every word.

The duke seemed to rally before he continued. "I made a bet many years ago that, unfortunately, Baronet Redgrove chose to take upon himself. Many of you know the outcome of that day and the resulting end to Miss Cooper's first Season due to her sustained injuries. It was never my intention for either Redgrove to be injured or Iris, but they were and my lack of consideration of them during that time is my burden to bear and burden to seek forgiveness for, if ever possible."

The guests did not speak, but the looks they passed between them told Iris some did not know his involvement. That some of the ladies present cast her knowing looks of glee did not pass her by either.

He went on. "What you are unaware of is that upon meeting Miss Cooper, plagued with guilt and the need to make her Season here this year one to remember, I somehow stumbled headlong in love with her. With every breath of my body, I wanted her. She was everything I did not want, or so I thought, and yet everything my soul craved. I could not sleep or eat without thinking of her." His eyes held hers, and Iris felt moisture pool in hers. Could he be saying all these things and before the entire London elite?

Surely he was not?

"I had to have her as my wife," he declared. "And so I took liberties that were not mine to take. I kissed her. That my mother came upon us was perfect for me, for honor demanded I ask her to be mine, and she agreed. While the last of my declaration sounds like I had no other choice, of course, I did. I did not have to offer anything. I could have spoken to the duchess and persuaded her to give over. But I did not want to."

The knowing looks changed to ones of envy, and Iris felt hope bloom within her soul. Like a warm ray of sunshine lit her body to life and renewed her spirit.

"I never asked you to marry me, Iris, because I felt sorry for you," he said, finding her in the crowd and holding her gaze. "Nor did I ask out of pity for your situation or my guilt over your circumstances. I merely used them at first to get close to you. I soon fell in love with your laughter, kindness, sweet, gentle soul that only ever wants the best for others. I want you as my duchess. No other lady will do." He shrugged, and she bit her lip, swallowing hard. She was on the verge of tears and before everyone who was anyone, but she did not care. No one else mattered but the duke—the man she loved.

She heard her grandmother sigh with pleasure before dabbing at her own damp cheeks at the duke's words.

Iris let go of her grandmother's hand and found the small flight of stairs leading up to Josh. Her steps slowed as she came toward him, the riveted visages of the orchestra musicians watching their every move.

"I assume by what you are saying, Your Grace, that you are sorry."

His shoulders sagged in relief, and he pulled her against him, tipping her face up for a kiss. The wanting of the man in her arms left her breathless, even with the *ton* looking on in awe. The scandalous gasps from the matrons of the *ton*, the shouts from men faded as the kiss continued.

Iris kissed him with everything she could, all the pent-up emotions she had fought this past week. The terror that she would remain heartbroken for the rest of her days living her life out in Cornwall a mean, old spinster. A woman haunted by the fear she had been played the fool by the man she loved.

"Marry me, Iris. You are my heart and soul. Forgive me and marry me, please." His voice soothed any remaining anxieties, and she nodded, knowing this was what she wanted. What she had always wanted from the very first moment her eyes had taken in the duke. There was only ever the duke.

"I will marry you, my heart."

Josh wrenched her against him again, their kiss, devastatingly slow, a dance of seduction and promise of what was to come in life, what she had to look forward to, days and nights of endless love and adoration. The kiss went on and on. Iris felt the familiar need to be with Josh alone thrum through her veins, and she reveled in it. She disregarded the *ton* watching them and kissed her husband to be. Soon she would be his, and he would be hers, and there was nothing that anyone or anything could do to change that fact.

"May I escort you home?" he asked her, a question in his stormy blue orbs that she understood.

"Take me back to your mother's home, Your Grace. I would prefer that."

A wicked grin lifted on his lips, and he started for the stairs. Iris having to run a little to keep up with him. She laughed, knowing they would be the scandal of the Season and the most talked of for many months to come. But she did not mind, for she had her husband to be, and the ton, for all she cared, could go hang their gossiping tongues. She was to be a duchess. There would be no pitying glances now. Nor ever again.

CHAPTER 32

*T*hey snuck away from the ball, and Iris wasn't naive enough not to know that both their families knew they were leaving, and together. They did not raise a brow when both declared they would like to depart, and with two carriages brought around the front of the townhouse, Iris hoped that no one else would notice their disappearance.

The duke's carriage pulled up at the front of the ducal townhouse while hers was taken around back to the mews. The footman guided her through the gardens, and she felt the tension leave her shoulders when Josh came to the terrace doors leading onto the gardens to escort her inside.

"I did not think I would ever see you grace this home again," he declared, wrapping his arm around her waist and giving her a comforting squeeze.

Iris's blood pumped fast through her veins, and she felt her nipples tighten, the longing between her legs increase. Since having been intimate with Josh, when apart from him, her need for him had only increased.

She had wondered if they were to be separated for the

remainder of their lives, however would she survive not being with him?

He guided her up the stairs, the house quiet but alight with candles, flowers everywhere just as it always was.

Josh walked them along the long corridor and past her own suite of rooms to come to his. She had not been in his room before and wondered what it was like.

It was unlike anything she had seen in her life. Iris felt her mouth gape at the ornate, painted ceiling. The large, four-poster mahogany bed had three steps leading up to the mattress itself, placing it higher than the rest of the room's furniture. Dark-blue silk bedding covered the bed, the settee before the fire, and the desk chair, all upholstered in the same color. The room sparkled with gold and rich blues and greens. The Aubusson rug underneath her silk slippers, opulent and soft.

This would be her room, too, when she shared his bed. "I cannot help but wonder what my suite of rooms will look like after seeing this one. Your bedroom is the most magnificent room I've ever seen in my life."

He chuckled, throwing his superfine coat over a nearby chair. Josh walked to the door, snipping the lock, and came toward her.

Iris swallowed, nervous for some reason but also excited for what was to come. He was so handsome, his eyes dark pools full of promise and need. She reached for him when he came close enough, wrapping her arms around his neck.

"Our bedroom, Duchess. Of course, you do have one of your own through those doors just there," he said, pointing across the room, "but I hope you spend most of your time in here. With me."

She kissed him quickly, needing to taste him again. Remind herself that this was real, and they were engaged again, but this time, without any secrets or hurts that could raise their ugly heads and destroy them.

His lips, soft at first, demanded more, and she was soon swept into a haze of desire. He kissed her hard, almost punishing her with his need, but she met his every want with those of her own. How she had missed him. Had wanted him so very much, even through the pain she endured this past week.

*H*is fingers worked the buttons of her gown quickly, slipping her dress from her shoulders to pool at her feet. Josh's blood pumped loud in his ears. He needed her, needed to know she was indeed here and his from this day forward.

Her fine shift that sat over her corset was almost transparent, and he could see the outline of her small stomach, the flaring of her hips. He wanted to kiss every inch of her. Mark and learn every part of her, declare that she was his and no one else's.

Josh untied the delicate ribbons on her shift, slipping that too from her body. He turned her about, his hands furiously working the stays. They, too, fell to the floor. Then, wanting to kiss her as much as his need to breathe, he whipped her about, taking her face in his hands and kissing her soundly.

She met his demand, her sweet tongue dancing with his, making his cock stand on end, weep with need for her.

He slid his hands down the soft skin of her back, feeling the small indentation from her stays before cupping her ass. He lifted her, pleased when she wrapped her legs about his hips and pressed against him, her wet cunny, hungry for him as much as he was for her.

He took the few steps to the bed, tumbling them onto the soft mattress and not bothering to pull down the bedding.

His need rode him hard, and he could not think straight for want of her.

"You're so beautiful," he declared, settling between her legs and rubbing himself along her slick, hot heat.

She gasped, her teeth pinning her bottom lip as he teased her. "I want you, Josh. Do not make me wait."

He grinned, dipping his head to kiss the sensitive spot just beneath her ear, her neck, and then down to her perfect-handful breasts. He took one into his mouth, laving her nipple, watching it with awe as it puckered farther at his touch.

He rolled her other nipple between his fingers, eliciting a moan from her lips. His cock twitched at the sound, and he knew he had to make her come before he went anywhere near her, or he'd spill before she gained her climax.

A man could only take so much, and he had thought she was lost to him. That never again would he have her in his arms. The knowledge and the realization she was here now, his and only his for the remainder of their lives, drove him to distraction. Made him lose any control he may have held.

"I will not, darling," he said, kissing her flat stomach, working his way out to her hip, nibbling and kissing his way between her thighs. She opened for him, and he marveled that she was so willing to do anything he wanted.

The jagged, red scar from her carriage accident came into view on her thigh, and he kissed his way along it. Iris ran her fingers into his hair, her hand soothing the guilt he would forever feel having written the bet that injured her.

"Josh," she moaned when he kissed the sensitive inner flesh of her thigh. He licked his lips, the sight of her wet, weeping cunny making his head spin. He pushed her legs apart, kissing her where she ached.

She gasped, her fingers spiking against his skull. He worked her flesh, kissed and tasted her need. She was sweet and musky, perfect in every way. She lifted her ass off the bed, seeking her pleasure. Josh reveled in her freedom, her womanly wiles that took what she wanted from him without fear or shame.

"You taste so sweet, my darling. I'm going to make you come so hard," he declared, his tongue mad against her engorged nubbin. He teased the opening of her sex before pushing two fingers into her hot heat. She shuddered at his intrusion, her body bucking at his touch.

She held his head against her flesh as the first tremors of her climax skittered through her core.

She called out his name, a chant as she took her pleasure. Josh laved at her flesh, wanting more, always wanting more of her.

He came atop her, her gaze luminous and pleased. Her legs wrapped about his hips, pulling him close.

He needed no encouragement. Josh thrust into her, unable to wait for a second longer. She gasped his name, brought him down for a kiss. He took her mouth, owned every part of it, mimicking what his cock was doing with his tongue.

His heart was full, his body alive and teetering on edge. He wanted her to come again but did not know if he could hold off. He pushed, deep, angling himself to tease her in a way he knew worked.

She reared up, grinding herself against him, and he lost his breath. Where had the little hellcat, the siren in his arms, come from? He adored this side of Iris, and that it was all for him, no one else would ever have her in such a way, was an elixir to his soul.

He took her relentlessly, and she shattered beneath him, her fingers scored down his back as she came for the second time in the night.

He promised it would not be her last as he lost himself

within her, a small part of him hoping that his seed would take root and they would start their family this evening.

He wanted all of her, forever and even longer than that, if he could negotiate with God. He slumped to her side, pulling her into the crook of his arm. Their breathing ragged, he smiled into the firelit room, content for the first time in what felt like a lifetime.

"I love you," she whispered, kissing his chest before promptly falling into a deep sleep.

Josh chuckled, kissing the top of her head. "I love and adore you, Duchess," he declared, unable to wait until he married her, which, if he could make use of the special license he'd procured, would be tomorrow.

CHAPTER 33

Their wedding was held in the drawing room the following morning at the London townhouse. The home was theirs now, Josh and Iris's, and Iris could not believe she was now the Duchess of Penworth, a wife and hopefully soon a mother to the duke's children.

He stood with his sisters, the five of them together, laughing and smiling, each different, but all of them the same somehow—the love, especially that they all had for one another evident on their visages if nothing else.

How lovely that her dearest husband came from such a supportive, loving clan. That her mama was a favorite of the dowager duchess also played in her favor, and she could foresee many enjoyable Christmases, Seasons, and birthdays in the future.

"Congratulations, my dearest Iris. If I have not said this before, let me say so again now how very happy I am that you are my son's chosen bride. The love of his life, if my estimation of him is accurate. Which, as his mother, I'm usually right."

Iris chuckled, kissing the dowager's cheeks. "I thank you

for welcoming me into your home, for allowing me to have such a successful second Season. I owe you everything, throwing me into the realm of Josh. I would not have met him otherwise."

The dowager shook her head, watching her children across the room. "I do not think that is the case. Soul mates have a way of finding each other. You were destined to be my son's wife, his love. I'm as certain of that as I was certain of my love match all those years ago."

Iris felt her eyes grow damp, and she blinked, not wanting to turn into a watering pot on one of the happiest days of her life. "I must ask for I have not come across her, but did you invite Lady Sophie this morning?"

The duchess pursed her lips as if she had tasted something sour. "We did not. Lady Jane and I laid to rest any inclinations the little minx had in gaining the title of duchess. She is safely stowed back in Hampshire until she can behave herself next year."

Iris laughed, not having known the dowager or her mama could be so commanding in society. Still, they were friends and were from two powerful families, so it was not so unlikely they would remove any impediment to their children's happiness.

"Thank you for your assistance with her. I was uncertain how to, if I'm honest," Iris admitted, having never liked conflict.

"You are most welcome," the dowager said, smiling as Josh walked up to them both. He bussed his mama on her cheek before reaching for Iris.

His large, strong arm wrapped about her waist, and she reveled in the public display of his affection that he had taken a liking to it would seem. Iris glanced about the parlor where the morning wedding breakfast was being hosted and noted several eyes had taken note of his hold. Iris smiled up at him.

"I have asked for Elizabeth to play a waltz on the pianoforte, Duchess. Will you do me the honor?" he asked her, his eyes warm and promising of the wonderful future they would have.

"I would love to dance, Your Grace."

Josh led her over to a part of the room that allowed a little dancing, and Elizabeth started to play. He pulled her into his arms, holding her closer than he ought for propriety's sake. Not that Iris would say anything about it. She adored being in his arms, being his.

"Happy, my darling?" His hand on her hip moved about her back and made little circular motions along the bottom of her spine. She shivered.

"I'm so happy, and you?" she asked him, wanting to hear him say it as well.

He leaned down, kissing her before everyone present. Iris felt heat kiss her cheeks, and she grinned like a debutante at her first ball when he pulled back.

Josh chuckled. "I have never been more so. The thought of a future, a life with you at my side, is a puzzle piece I never knew I was missing. Not until I met you." He kissed her again as he turned them about. "I intend on making you so very happy until I take my last breath, Your Grace."

Iris's eyes smarted, and she blinked, trying to clear her vision, but it was no use. His sweet declaration, the way he looked at her now, as if she were everything to him. His sun and moon, the breath that he breathed, his reason for living were too much to endure. She would never have enough of him.

She sniffed. "I'm pleased that you promise me such things, for I adore you too. So much. I never want to be parted from you ever again. I could not bear it."

Josh swung them to a stop, cupping her face and wiping the stray tears from her cheeks. "We will never be divided again. If it is the one promise I make, know that to be true and steadfast."

Iris nodded, knowing he would hold to his decree. Had she not been so caught up in her husband's love and warmth, she would have noticed the room stood in awe, in envy, and without a dry eye in the room at the love shared by the Duke and Duchess of Penworth.

The devotion.

EPILOGUE

Three years later

Iris sat on a daybed in their private suite of rooms, staring out at the gardens of Dunsleigh. She watched as her husband walked about the roses with their gardener, gesturing his plans for a new design and layout to the beds.

She smiled, running a hand over her very pregnant belly, the fear that something was wrong never far from her mind. She was uncommonly large and had been from the first moment they found out she was expecting.

At first, Iris had put it down to too much cheese and bacon at breakfast that she had craved, and then followed by turtle soup and soufflé. But she could no longer say such things. Every time any of Josh's sisters visited, each of them exclaimed over her size, happy, but even she could see the concern that clouded their vision.

She rolled to her side, a cushion beneath her stomach for support, and gasped as a rush of fluid spilled from between her legs and onto the daybed.

Iris shuffled to the side, gaining her feet, and walked carefully to the bellpull, relieved when her lady's maid bustled in with a fresh pot of tea and biscuits.

"Becky, please have the doctor come immediately and fetch the duke. I think I'm going to have the baby today."

For a moment her maid, wide-eyed, did not move. She merely looked as stunned as Iris was when the fluid gave way before she rallied and all but threw the tray down on a nearby table and bolted out of the room.

Iris smiled, having never seen her move so fast in her life. She made her way over to her bed, ready to settle herself under the blankets when her husband, his face pale but his eyes alight with expectation, stumbled into the room, rushing to her side to assist her.

"Iris darling. Your maid said you think you're in labor?"

She nodded, pointing to a pile of folded cloths on a nearby chair that was standing in wait for this very day. "Those linens, Josh. Grab them quickly. I'm leaking fluid all over the bed."

He glanced at her wet gown and did as she bade, coming back to her with all the linens in hand. "Would you like me to place one under you?" he asked her, ripping the bedding down and out of the way.

"Yes, I think that is best. When the doctor arrives, I'm certain he will help us further."

The maid came into the room, less harried and accompanied by their housekeeper who had birthed many babies over the years, Josh one of those children.

She dipped into a curtsy, coming over to Iris. "Your Graces, it looks as if the day has arrived. The doctor has been sent for by our fastest rider, Jeffrey, but I think it is best if we strip Her Grace of her gown and down to her shift where she will be more comfortable."

Iris nodded, and then a wrenching pain tore through her,

stealing her breath. She reached for Josh, the fear in his eyes echoing her own at what she was enduring. The pain grew, her stomach cramped, and she screamed, clasping her body in the hopes that it would stop.

It did not. "Josh, it hurts. I can't."

"You can," he said, taking her hand and kissing it. "You are so brave and strong. The strongest woman I know. I know you can, and you will. Just keep breathing, my love."

The housekeeper quickly did away with Iris's gown, and she lay back against a bank of pillows that Josh had placed behind her, giving her as much comfort as he could.

But it was no use. The pain would not cease, and each time it seemed to become longer, more painful until it felt as if it were one continuous spasm.

Sweat poured off her in droves. Josh dabbed a damp cloth on her brow, but it was too much. Too soon. She wasn't ready to have a baby. She had been told labor was a slow process that increased over hours. She could not bear it if that were true of her situation, and it only became worse than it already was.

Pain tore through her again, and she felt the urge to push. The housekeeper lifted her shift, her eyes widening. Iris did not know what to make of that and nor could she voice her question as another cramp tore through her abdomen, robbing her of her wits.

"What is it?" Josh demanded, a fierce glare on his brow.

"The baby. It's crowning." The housekeeper settled at the end of the bed. "Your Grace, you're going to have this baby without the doctor present, but do not fear, I see the head and have helped birth many babes, your husband one of them. I shall keep you safe."

Iris did not miss the whispered words of her husband, who murmured *you better* before coming to sit beside Iris, supporting her as best he could. She held on to him, needing his support more than ever. She clasped his hands as another cramp wrenched her abdomen, and she again felt the urge to push.

She did as the housekeeper bade, bearing down, wanting the child out if only to end this unenduring agony. "Josh," she sobbed, unable to hide the panic in her voice. "Please help me. I can't do it."

"Push, darling. Push out our child."

She did as he bade, pushing with all her might, and a wail sounded from the end of the bed. Iris heaved a sigh of relief, flopping back onto the cushions. The sight of the house-keeper holding up the small pink babe made her lose control of her emotions, and she sobbed, reaching out to take the baby.

The housekeeper laid the babe upon her, tying the cord that connected Iris to the baby twice before cutting it free.

Iris lifted the baby's little leg and smiled. "It's a girl, Josh. We have a daughter."

She looked up at her husband and found his eyes full of tears, his cheeks wet with emotion. She tried to comfort him, but she did not feel any better. Pain ripped through her a second time, and she gasped, handing the baby off to Josh.

The housekeeper who was cleaning her hands rushed back over to her and checked her. "Oh, Your Grace."

"What?" Josh yelled, handing the child over to Iris's lady's maid.

The housekeeper settled at the base of the bed again. "I believe another baby is coming."

"What?" Iris and Josh said in unison before Josh came over to her again when she reached for him.

"How can there be another? The doctor never stated as much," Josh demanded as if it were the housekeeper's fault.

"It happens sometimes. A baby will hide behind the other in the womb."

Iris cringed as the awful, ripping pain wracked her body, and again the urge to push assailed her. She bore down, determined to birth a second child in as many minutes. At this point, determination kicked in, and she wanted it over. Never again would she birth another child. It was too much. Too awful for words, even if her daughter was the prettiest little cherub to exist.

"I see the head," the housekeeper declared.

With all her might, Iris pushed when the next contraction assailed her. She did not know if she was doing it right or if she was making any progress. For what seemed like longer than the first, she worked on getting her next baby born.

Another contraction, another urge, and with what was left of her strength, she pushed hard and was relieved when a second piercing cry rent the air, marking the second child was alive and well.

As before, the housekeeper laid the baby on her chest, the little dark-haired sweetheart so similar to their first.

"Josh met her gaze, his face tear-streaked, the tip of his nose red. "It's a boy," he stated, grinning.

Becky brought over their daughter and placed her too in Iris's arms. She stared down at her children, their children, and could not have felt her heart more full.

The din of racing horse's hooves sounded on the gravel outside. Within a few minutes, the doctor ran into the room, bag in hand and face aghast at seeing that the Duchess of Penworth already birthed her children.

"Your Graces, congratulations," he said, coming over to them and looking down at the children.

Josh gestured to their housekeeper. "Mrs. Morris had it all in hand, but I thank you for attending us on such short notice."

"Well," the doctor said, smiling at Mrs. Morris, "sometimes these things do occur quite quickly. Let me see how the duchess fares and the children, and then I shall leave you in peace."

The doctor ensured she birthed what he called the after-birth and checked over the children before leaving them in peace. Telling them that he would prefer to sleep at the estate that night just in case any complications arose.

Josh was more than satisfied at having the doctor so close by, but Iris knew she was past the most dangerous part of the birth. She felt well, and after removing herself to the duke's bed, in fresh clothing and her children bathed, she was safely and comfortably ensconced in their bed, their babies sleeping soundly between them.

"I cannot believe we have two," she said for the hundredth time, unable to stop staring at what looked to be identical little faces.

Josh ran a hand over his son's cheek and then reached down and kissed both their children's foreheads. "I cannot believe it either. How talented you are, my darling wife."

"I do believe you had a role to play in my cleverness." Iris chuckled, leaning over for her own kiss from her husband.

"We're a family now," he declared, so much pride and love basking from his every pore.

Iris could not contain her grin. "I know, but with children or not, we were always a family. We're now simply a bigger one."

"You are right, as always."

"Talking of family, I do believe I hear your mama and sister Alice."

Josh cocked his head to the side, nodding just as the door burst open and in flocked not only the dowager duchess but Alice, Elizabeth, Isolde, and Victoria, recently returned for a time from abroad.

Josh gestured them over. "Come and meet our children," he said, the tenor of his voice proud and thick with emotion.

Each sister took turns in kissing them both before gushing over the little babies asleep in the bed.

"The future of the Penworth family continues. How proud of you I am, my son, and you, my darling Iris."

Iris clasped Josh's hand, squeezing it in support. She glanced down at her small boy, the future Duke of Penworth, and his sister, already a lady by birth. Two little beings with such a plentiful and full life ahead of them.

Alice handed them each a glass of champagne, where from, Iris had no idea but welcomed the bubbly, refreshing drink.

Alice raised her glass. "To the Worthingham family and Duke of Penworth line. May we thrive for years to come. May our children prosper and have loves as grand as ours have been. Have full and happy lives."

Iris raised her glass. "To family and love."

The others followed. "To us," Josh said, sipping his champagne and reaching for her. Iris kissed him, her heart incredibly full and happy. *To us indeed*, she thought. *To us all.*

Dear Reader,

I hope you enjoyed, *Only a Lady Will Do*, book five in my To Marry a Rogue series!

I'm so thrilled you chose my book to read, and if you're able, I would appreciate an honest review of *Only a Lady Will Do*. As they say, feed an author, leave a review!

If you'd like to learn about book one in my To Marry a Rogue series, *Only an Earl Will Do*, please read on. I have included the prologue for your reading pleasure.

Alternatively, you can keep in contact with me by visiting my website or following me online. You can contact me at www.tamaragill.com or email me at tamaragillauthor@gmail.com.

Tamara Gill

ONLY AN EARL WILL DO

TO MARRY A ROGUE, BOOK 1

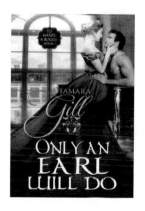

*The reigning queen of London society, Lady Elizabeth Worthing-
ham, has her future set out for her. Marry well, and marry without
love. An easy promise to make and one she owed her family after
her near ruinous past that threatened them all. And the rakish
scoundrel Henry Andrews, Earl of Muir who's inability to act a
gentleman when she needed one most would one day pay for his
treachery.*

. . .

Returning to England after three years abroad, Henry is determined to make the only woman who captured his heart his wife. But the icy reception he receives from Elizabeth is colder than his home in the Scottish highlands. As past hurts surface and deception runs as thick as blood, so too does a love that will overcome all obstacles, unless a nameless foe, determined with his own path, gets his way and their love never sees the light of day...

PROLOGUE

England 1805 – Surrey

"You're ruined."

Elizabeth stood motionless as her mother, the Duchess of Penworth, paced before the lit hearth, her golden silk gown billowing out behind her, the deep frown between her eyes daring anyone to follow her. "No. Let me rephrase that. The family is ruined. All my girls, their futures, have been kicked to the curb like some poor street urchins."

Elizabeth, the eldest of all the girls, swiped a lone tear from her cheek and fought not to cast up her accounts. "But surely Henry has written of his return." She turned to her father. "Papa, what did his missive say?" The severe frown lines between her father's brows were deeper than she'd ever seen them before, and dread pooled in her belly. What had she done? What had Henry said?

"I shall not read it to you, Elizabeth, for I fear it'll only upset you more, and being in the delicate condition you are we must keep you well. But never again will I allow the Earl of Muir to step one foot into my home. To think," her father said, kicking at a log beside the fire, "that I supported him to seek out his uncle in America. I'm utterly ashamed of myself."

"No," Elizabeth said, catching her father's gaze. "You have nothing to be ashamed of. I do. I'm the one who lay with a man who wasn't my husband. I'm the one who now carries his child." The tears she'd fought so hard to hold at bay started to run in earnest. "Henry and I were friends, well, I thought we were friends. I assumed he'd do the right thing by our family, by me. Why is it that he'll not return?"

Her mother, quietly staring out the window, turned at her question. "Because his uncle has said no nephew of his would marry a strumpet who gave away the prize before the contracts were signed, and Henry apparently was in agreement with this statement."

Her father sighed. "There is an old rivalry between Henry's uncle and me. We were never friends, even though I noted Henry's father high in my esteem, as close as a brother, in fact. Yet his sibling was temperamental, a jealous cur."

"Why were you not friends with Henry's uncle, Papa?" He did not reply. "Please tell me. I deserve to know."

"Because he wished to marry your mama, and I won her hand instead. He was blind with rage, and it seems even after twenty years he wishes to seek revenge upon me by ruining you."

Elizabeth flopped onto a settee, shocked by such news. "Did Henry know of this between you and his uncle? Did you ever tell him?"

"No. I thought it long forgotten."

Elizabeth swallowed as the room started to swirl. "So, Henry has found his wealthy uncle and has been poisoned by his lies. The man has made me out to be a light-skirts of little character." She took a calming breath. "Tell me, does the letter really declare this to be Henry's opinion as well?"

The duke came and sat beside her. "It is of both their opinions, yes." He took her hand and squeezed it. "You need to marry, Elizabeth, and quickly. There is no other choice."

She stood, reeling away from her father and such an idea. To marry a stranger was worse than no marriage at all and falling from grace. "I cannot do that. I haven't even had a season. I know no one."

"A good friend of mine, Viscount Newland, recently passed. His son, Marcus, who is a little simple of mind after a fall from a horse as a child, is in need of a wife. But because of his ailment, no one will have him. They are desperate to keep the estate within the family and are looking to marry him off. It would be a good match for you both. I know it is not what you wanted, but it will save you and your sisters from ruin."

Elizabeth stood looking down at her father, her mouth agape with shock and not a little amount of disgrace. "You want me to marry a simpleton?"

"His speech is a little delayed only, otherwise he's a kind young man. I grant you he's not as handsome as Henry, but... well, we must do what's best in these situations."

Her mother sighed. "Lord Riddledale has called and asked for your hand once more. You could always accept his suit."

"Please, I would rather cut off my own hand than marry his lordship." Just the thought was enough to make her skin crawl.

"Well then, you will marry Lord Newland. I'm sorry, but it must and will be done," her mother said, her tone hard.

Elizabeth walked to the window that looked toward the lake where she'd given herself to Henry. His sweet whispered words of love, of wanting her to wait for him, that as soon as he procured enough funds to support his Scottish estate they would marry, flittered through her mind. What a liar he'd turned out to be. All he wanted was her innocence and nothing else.

Anger thrummed through her and she grit her teeth. How dare Henry trick her in such a way? Made her fall in love with him, promised to be faithful and marry her when he returned. He never wished to marry her. Had he wanted to right now he would be on his way back to England.

She turned, staring at her parents who looked resigned to a fate none of them imagined possible or ever wanted. "I will marry Viscount Newland. Write them and organize the nuptials to take place within the month or sooner if possible. The child I carry needs a father and the viscount needs a wife."

"Then it is done." Her father stood, walking over to her and taking her hand. "Did Henry promise you anything, Elizabeth? The letter is so out of character for him, I've wondered since receiving it that it isn't really of his opinion but his uncle's only."

"He wanted me to wait for him, to give him time to save his family's estate. He did not wish to marry a woman for her money; he wanted to be a self-made man, I suppose."

"Lies, Elizabeth. All lies," her mother stated, her voice cold. "Henry has used you, I fear, and I highly doubt he'll ever come back to England or Scotland, for that matter."

Elizabeth swallowed the lump in her throat, not wanting to believe the man she'd given her heart to would treat her in such a way. She'd thought Henry was different, was a gentleman who loved her. At the look of pity her father bestowed on her, she pushed him aside and ran from the room.

She needed air, fresh, cooling, calming air. Opening the front door, the chilling icy wind hit her face, and clarity assailed. She'd go for a ride. Her mount Argo always made her feel better.

It took the stable hand only minutes to saddle her mount, and she was soon trotting away from the house, the only sound that of the snow crunching beneath her horse's hooves. The chill pierced through her gown, and she regretted not changing into a suitable habit, but riding astride in whatever they had on at the time was a normal practice for the children of the Duke of Penworth. Too much freedom as a child, all of them allowed to do whatever they pleased, and now that freedom had led her straight into the worst type of trouble.

She pushed her horse into a slow canter, her mind a kaleidoscope of turmoil. Henry, once her father's ward, a person she'd thought to call a friend, had betrayed her when she needed him most. Guilt and shame swamped her just as snow started to fall, and covered everything in a crystal white hue.

She would never forgive Henry for this. Yes, they'd made a mistake, a terrible lack of decorum on her behalf that she'd never had time to think through. But should the worst happen, a child, she had consoled herself that Henry would do right by her, return home and marry her.

How could she have been so wrong?

She clutched her stomach, still no signs that a little child grew inside, and as much as she was ruined, could possibly ruin her family, she didn't regret her condition, and nor would she birth this child out of wedlock. Lord Newland would marry her since his situation was not looked upon favorably by the ton; it was a match that would suit them both.

Guilt pricked her soul that she would pass off Henry's child as Lord Newland's, but what choice did she have? Henry would not marry her, declare the child his. Elizabeth had little choice. There was nothing else to be done about it.

A deer shot out of the bracken, and Argo shied, jumping

sharply to the side. Elizabeth screamed as her seat slipped. The action unbalanced her and she fell, hitting the ground hard.

Luckily, the soft snow buffered her fall, and she sat up, feeling the same as she had when upon her horse. She rubbed her stomach, tears pooling in her eyes with the thought that had she fallen harder, all her problems would be over. What a terrible person she was to think such a thing, and how she hated Henry that his refusal of her had brought such horrendous thoughts to mind.

Argo nuzzled her side as she stood; reaching for the stirrup, she hoisted herself back onto her mount. Wiping the tears from her eyes, Elizabeth promised no more would be shed over a boy, for that was surely what Henry still was, an immature youth who gave no thought to others.

She would marry Viscount Newland, try and make him happy as much as possible when two strangers came together in such a union, and be damned anyone who mentioned the name Henry Andrews, Lord Muir to her again.

America 1805 – New York Harbor

Henry raised his face to the wind and rain as the packet ship sailed up the Hudson River. The damp winter air matched the cold he felt inside, numbing the pain that hadn't left his core since farewelling the shores of England. And now he was here. America. The smoky city just waking to a new day looked close enough to reach out and touch, and yet his true love, Elizabeth, was farther away than she'd ever been before.

He rubbed his chest and huddled into his greatcoat. The

five weeks across the ocean had dragged, endless days with his mind occupied with only one thought: his Elizabeth lass.

He shut his eyes, bringing the vision of her to his mind, her honest, laughing gaze, the beautiful smile that had always managed to make his breath catch. He frowned, missing her as much as the highland night sky would miss the stars.

"So, Henry, lad, what's your plan on these great lands?" Henry took in the captain on the British Government packet; his graying whiskers across his jaw and crinkled skin about his eyes told of a man who'd lived at sea his entire life, and enjoyed every moment of it. He grinned. "Make me fortune. Mend a broken family tie if I can."

The captain lit a cheroot and puffed, the smoke soon lost in the misty air. "Ah, grand plans then. Any ideas on how you'll be making your fortune? I could use some tips myself."

"My uncle lives here. Owns a shipping company apparently, although I've yet to meet the man or see for myself if this is true. I'm hoping since he's done so well for himself he can steer me along the road to me own fortune."

The captain nodded, staring toward the bow. "It seems you have it all covered."

Henry started when the captain yelled orders for half-mast. He hoped the old man was right with his statement. The less time he stayed here the better it would be. He pushed away the thought that Elizabeth was due to come out in the forthcoming months, to be paraded around the ton like a delicious morsel of sweet meats. To be the center of attention, a duke's daughter ripe for the picking. He ground his teeth.

"I wish you good luck, Henry."

"Thank ye." The captain moved away, and he turned back to look at the city so unlike London or his highland home. Foreign and wrong on so many levels. The muddy waters were the only similarity to London, he mused, smiling a little.

Henry walked to the bow, leaning over the wooden rail. He sighed, trying to expel the sullen mood that had swamped him the closer they came to America. What he was doing here was a good thing, an honorable thing, something that if he didn't do, Elizabeth would be lost to him forever.

He couldn't have hated his grandfather more at that moment for having lost their fortune at the turn of a card all those years ago. It was a miracle his father had been able to keep Avonmore afloat and himself out of debtor's prison.

The crewmen preparing the packet ship for docking sounded around him, and he started toward the small room he'd been afforded for the duration of the trip. It was better than nothing; even if he'd not been able to stand up fully within the space, at least it was private and comfortable.

Determination to succeed, to ensure his and Elizabeth's future was secure, to return home as soon as he may, sparked within him. He would not fail; for once, the Earl of Muir would not gamble the estate's future away, but fight for its survival, earn it respectably just as his ancestors had.

And he would return home, marry his English lass, and spoil her for the remainder of their days. In Scotland.

Want to read more? Purchase Only an Earl Will Do here!

LORDS OF LONDON SERIES
AVAILABLE NOW!

Dive into these charming historical romances! In this six-book series, Darcy seduces a virginal duke, Cecilia's world collides with a roguish marquess, Katherine strikes a deal with an unlucky earl and Lizzy sets out to conquer a very wicked Viscount. These stories plus more adventures in the Lords of London series! Available now through Amazon or read free with KindleUnlimited.

Lords of London

KISS THE WALLFLOWER SERIES
AVAILABLE NOW!

If the roguish Lords of London are not for you and wall-flowers are more your cup of tea, this is the series for you. My Kiss the Wallflower series, are linked through friendship and family in this four-book series. You can grab a copy on Amazon or read free through KindleUnlimited.

LEAGUE OF UNWEDDABLE GENTLEMEN SERIES AVAILABLE NOW!

Fall into my latest series, where the heroines have to fight for what they want, both regarding their life and love. And where the heroes may be unweddable to begin with, that is until they meet the women who'll change their fate. The League of Unweddable Gentlemen series is available now!

LEAGUE OF UNWEDDABLE GENTLEMEN

Lords of London Series

TO BEDEVIL A DUKE

TO MADDEN A MARQUESS

TO TEMPT AN EARL

TO VEX A VISCOUNT

TO DARE A DUCHESS

TO MARRY A MARCHIONESS

LORDS OF LONDON - BOOKS 1-3 BUNDLE

LORDS OF LONDON - BOOKS 4-6 BUNDLE

To Marry a Rogue Series

ONLY AN EARL WILL DO

ONLY A DUKE WILL DO

ONLY A VISCOUNT WILL DO

ONLY A MARQUESS WILL DO

ONLY A LADY WILL DO

TO MARRY A ROGUE - BOOKS 1-5 BUNDLE

A Time Traveler's Highland Love Series

TO CONQUER A SCOT

TO SAVE A SAVAGE SCOT

TO WIN A HIGHLAND SCOT

HIGHLAND LOVE - BOOKS 1-3 BUNDLE

A Stolen Season Series

A STOLEN SEASON

A STOLEN SEASON: BATH

A STOLEN SEASON: LONDON

Time Travel Romance

DEFIANT SURRENDER

Scandalous London Series
A GENTLEMAN'S PROMISE
A CAPTAIN'S ORDER
A MARRIAGE MADE IN MAYFAIR
SCANDALOUS LONDON - BOOKS 1-3 BUNDLE

High Seas & High Stakes Series
HIS LADY SMUGGLER
HER GENTLEMAN PIRATE
HIGH SEAS & HIGH STAKES - BOOKS 1-2 BUNDLE

Daughters Of The Gods Series
BANISHED-GUARDIAN-FALLEN
DAUGHTERS OF THE GODS - BOOKS 1-3 BUNDLE

Stand Alone Books
TO SIN WITH SCANDAL
OUTLAWS

ABOUT THE AUTHOR

Tamara is an Australian author who grew up in an old mining town in country South Australia, where her love of history was founded. So much so, she made her darling husband travel to the UK for their honeymoon, where she dragged him from one historical monument and castle to another.

A mother of three, her two little gentlemen in the making, a future lady (she hopes) and a part-time job keep her busy in the real world, but whenever she gets a moment's peace she loves to write romance novels in an array of genres, including regency, medieval and time travel.

www.tamaragill.com
tamaragillauthor@gmail.com

10684687R00144